LADY OF ROANOKE

LADY OF ROANOKE

BY JEAN BOTHWELL

Holt, Rinehart and Winston

NEW YORK · CHICAGO · SAN FRANCISCO

COPYRIGHT © 1965 BY JEAN BOTHWELL · ALL RIGHTS RE-
SERVED, INCLUDING THE RIGHT TO REPRODUCE THIS BOOK OR
PORTIONS THEREOF IN ANY FORM · PUBLISHED SIMULTANE-
OUSLY IN CANADA BY HOLT, RINEHART AND WINSTON OF CANADA,
LIMITED · LIBRARY OF CONGRESS CATALOG CARD NUMBER:
65-13867 · FIRST EDITION · 91034-0215 · PRINTED IN THE
UNITED STATES OF AMERICA

For Miss Mary Livermore,
friend, advocate, and
counselor of Lost Colony
descendants at Pembroke,
in Robeson County,
North Carolina—
with great admiration

The author wishes to acknowledge particularly the interested encouragement and material help received from Dr. Ralph A. Wellons, President (retired) of Pembroke College, Mrs. Wellons, and Miss Marjorie Kanable, the College librarian, in addition to the use of Miss Mary Livermore's private collection of historical data.

FOREWORD

The effort of a novelist to clothe history's bare bones must rely heavily upon known facts for proof that the story could have happened as portrayed. This book spans the years when Virginia Dare might have been growing up, from the age of three until she is mature enough to think about marriage.

Her fate, along with her parents and the other men and women who briefly appeared as themselves on history's stage in 1587, and then disappeared as a group some time between that date and 1591, has been a popular pursuit of mystery-probers for two hundred years and more.

Briefly, as one historian concludes his dissertation, after proving his theory to his own satisfaction—and to many who agree with him—*the colony wasn't necessarily lost just because its people were never found.*

Perhaps they wanted to disappear. The question is still debatable.

While we'd like to think that they were all cultured people, as the several Patentees of Sir Walter Raleigh's project undoubtedly were (if in varying degree), there were as surely others—those classed by Sir Humphrey Gilbert (who advocated colonization as much for its own sake as for the Queen's) as *needy people who troubled the commonwealth*. And added to these two groups were the adventurers, not all gentlemen in the old-fashioned swashbuckling meaning of the word, who may have found it quite convenient to leave home and for whom the lure of gold, reported to be had for the taking, and not colonization for Queen and country, was paramount.

The colonists thought they were coming to Chesapeake Bay in Virginia—named so by Queen Elizabeth I. Instead, because their pilot, Simon Ferdinando, refused to let the captain sail farther, they were landed on Roanoke Island, where they had expected to stop only to take on any possible survivors of an earlier attempt at settlement. The island is separated from the coast of present-day North Carolina by Croatan Sound.

They found no former colonists alive on the island, only some ruined houses and a fort, which they repaired and settled in, faring better than they might have, because one of the ship's list was Manteo, a young Indian who had been presented at court by Captain Grenville and who understood and could speak English.

Manteo was a Coree of the Hatteras Indians, Algonquin stock, and his people were living near Roanoke at the time the colonists arrived on Croatan Island. But *croatan* was the Indians' general term for their home country, a large part of the eastern mainland, extending as far south as Cape Fear.

Virginia Dare was born on August 18 that year of 1587,

the first child of colonist parents anywhere in the New World. Her naming is obvious.

When the ship that had brought the colony to Roanoke returned to England, John White, Governor of the new colony, and father of Eleanor Dare, was on board, going back to seek more and different supplies which would be far better suited to the physical situation at Roanoke than those they had brought for life on Chesapeake Bay.

His return to Virginia was delayed and when he came back in 1591 he found the houses wrecked, his own boxes, which he had thought safely buried, opened and the contents spoiled. He had known before he left that the colonists *were prepared to remove from Roanoke fifty miles into the main.* Yet the only direction to guide him to their new location was the word *Croatan* on a blazed tree. They had agreed to add a cross to the sign if they had been forced to leave by misadventure but there was no cross.

There are no known records made by the colonists themselves except John White's drawings and his later written reports. The chief resource materials have been the logs of the several ships' captains who brought colonists to the New World, the writings of the indefatigable Richard Hakluyt, geographer and historian, and those of Thomas Harriot, a young surveyor who went to Virginia in 1585 with the first English colony. Other accounts, known to have been made at the time, were carelessly lost, which is still deplorable after all the years between.

John White was a draughtsman and an artist, and, the first painter to do so, made maps and beautiful water color drawings of the Indians, their houses and ceremonies and of bird and fish life in the vicinity of Roanoke, seen on his several travels to the New World. He is known to have been with the company of Sir Walter's first colony in 1585. After twenty-three of the drawings were chosen to be engraved for illustration of a book, *The English Colony in*

Virginia, published in 1590, the rest of the drawings disappeared for almost two hundred years, but they are now preserved in the British Museum, still the principal source of pictorial material about pre-colonial Indian life.

Governor White's account of his search—his last, a letter to Richard Hakluyt written from Ireland in 1593 and after that never more heard from by anyone—shows him inclined to gloss over some of his mistaken conclusions after unintelligent action when he did return to Virginia. It has since been pointed out by weather experts that the violent tides and storms on the Outer Banks of the North Carolina coast could have shifted the sands and changed the shapes of islands, even confusing their relationship to each other. But even if he had found Croatan Island, to recognize it, would he have found his people? Historians think not.

From the safe and superior position of hindsight it is apparent today that White's misunderstanding of the full meaning of the word *croatan* is the key to his failure. Plus the possibility that the sign was meant to be misleading. That, and the reluctance of ship captain or pilot to wait upon a real search inland. Plain reasoning should have proved to him that settlers, afraid of unfriendly Indians on the seacoast and of Spanish marauders by sea, would not remove to another spot fairly close by, having the same hazards. Clearly to us, the anxious, discouraged colonists, shepherded by Manteo's people, left Roanoke and went home with them.

*Names of All the Men, Women and Children
which Safely Arrived in Virginia
and remained to inhabit there, 1587.
Anno Regni Reginae Elizabethae 29.*

Historical references do not present the names of the potential colonists in alphabetical order, though the groupings are similar, which obliges one to conclude that a man's place on the list had something to do with his status or occupation.

They are here grouped alphabetically for the sake of readers' easier reference to characters in the book.

Two lists attributed to Richard Hakluyt—the above caption is his—are not alike and they both differ from John White's report. There are variations in spellings of both given and surnames and in the case of children who do not seem to be with parents, one has a choice of decision, either they were nephews of some member of the company or the surname was not written. The absence of a second *t* in *Hewet, Prat* and *Scot,* and in *Bennet* on one list, is notable because we are used to double *t*. Also, though we are assured again and again that twelve of the seventeen women were married the decision as to who they were is baffling on account of the variation of surname spelling in the two adult groups. All these discrepancies must surely have been the fault of copyists.

THE MEN

Maurice Allen
Arnold Archard
Richard Arthur

Roger Bayly
Mark Bennett
William Berde
Henry Berry
Richard Berry
Michael Bishop
John Borden
John Bridger
John Bright
John Brooke
Henry Browne
William Browne
John Burden
Thomas Butler

Anthony Cage
John Chapman
John Cheven
William Clement
Thomas Colman
Christopher Cooper
John Cotsmur

Ananias Dare
Richard Darige
Henry Dorrell
William Dutton

John Earnest
Thomas Ellis
Edmond English

John Farre

Simon Ferdinando
Charles Florrie

John Gibbes
Thomas Gramme

Thomas Harris
Dionys Harvie
John Hemmington
Thomas Hewet
George Howe
James Hynde

Henry Johnson
Nicholas Johnson
Griffen Jones
John Jones

Richard Kemme

James Lasie
Peter Little
Robert Little
William Lucas

George Martyn
Michael Myllet
Henry Mylton

Humfrey Newton
William Nichols

Hugh Patterson
Henry Payne
Thomas Phevens
Edward Powell
Roger Prat

Henry Rufoote

John Sampson

Thomas Scot
Richard Shabedge
Thomas Smith
William Sole
John Starte
Thomas Stevens
John Stilman
Martin Sutton

Richard Taverner
Hugh Tayler
Clement Taylor
Richard Tomkins
Thomas Topan
John Tydway

Ambrose Viccars

Thomas Warner
William Waters
Cuthbert White
John White
Richard Wildye
Robert Wilkinson
William Willes
Lewes Wotton
John Wright
Brian Wyles
John Wyles

THE WOMEN

Joyce Archard
Alice Chapman
Eleanor Dare
Elizabeth Glane
Margery Harvie
Jane Jones

Margaret Lawrence
Jane Mannering
Emma Merrimoth
Rose Payne
Jane Pierce
Wenefred Powell
Audrey Tappan
Elizabeth Viccars
Joan Warren—or Warner?
Agnes Wood—or Wotton?

THE CHILDREN

Thomas Archard
Robert Ellis
Georgie Howe
Thomas Humfrey
John Prat
John Sampson
Thomas Smart
Ambrose Viccars
William Wythers
   Later:
Virginia Dare

THE PATENTEES

John White
Ananias Dare
Roger Bayly
Christopher Cooper
Humfrey Dimmocke
Dionys Harvie
John Nichols
Roger Prat
John Sampson
Thomas Stevens

CHARACTERS

VIRGINIA DARE, *Lady of Roanoke*
ANANIAS DARE, her father, and Chief Patentee of Sir Walter
  Raleigh's colony first settled on Roanoke Island, Virginia
ELEANOR DARE, her mother, daughter of John White, a
  Patentee absent in England
HUMPHREY HALL, a lad from Gilling Manor in Yorkshire
JOHN BROOKE, a Rector of the Church of England
GEORGIE HOWE, an orphan, aged eight, living with the Dares

  Prominent Colonists:
  Elizabeth Glane ⎫
  Jane Mannering ⎬ *Spinsters*
  Emma Merrimoth ⎭
  Dion and Margery Harvie

Henry Berry, blacksmith, and his wife, Jane Pierce, with three young sons

Thomas Warner, an Oxford Scholar, and Joan, his wife

Ambrose Viccars, his wife Elizabeth, Little Amby, almost six, and Ann

Tom-the-Lute Jones, a Welsh sailor, and his wife Margaret Lawrence, with Megan and Arthur, their children

Mark Bennett, carpenter and bachelor

Roger Prat, a Patentee, widower, and his young son, Johnnie, aged six

John Sampson and Billy Wythers, two almost-fourteens

The Indians, Corees of Algonquin stock:

Manteo

Mary, his mother

Felicity, his sister

Oppy, his cousin and god-of-the-machine for Virginia

CONTENTS

LADY OF ROANOKE

TO GO OR STAY?

1

The scuppernong grapes were ripe again on Roanoke's white beaches by early July of the year 1590.

Young Virginia Dare would not be three until mid-August, yet it was already noted by her anxious mother that the child sensed the special position she held in the colony and made the most of it—the only girl in a crowd of little boys.

Summertime was especially lovely on the island that year. The weather had been open and sunny for several weeks. Now the warm air was heavy with the fragrance of the fruit hanging in plump bunches on the low-growing vines, enhanced by the salt smell of the sea.

Lady of Roanoke

And while the gold Sir Walter Raleigh had sent the colonists to discover had not been found, there were other more successful aspects of their situation.

Their houses were in good repair. They had built a fort and a chapel. Their food was reasonably plentiful, from gardens and the Viccars' cows and the blue sea waters all about. No one was ill. In sum, they had only two clouds in their sky—the absence of the gold was a small one but the other was growing larger every day and that was the absence of their Governor, John White, father of Eleanor Dare, and his delayed return from England where he had gone hopefully to procure supplies. He meant to bring back warmer clothing, more furniture, blankets and small tools, all of which would help the colonists adapt to island life. They had originally planned to establish new homes inland near Chesapeake Bay where the climate was less rugged.

It was almost eleven o'clock on a lovely morning toward the end of July's first week when Humphrey Hall, the orphan lad who had run away from his family manor, Gilling in Yorkshire, to join Sir Walter Raleigh's colonists sailing to the New World, came scurrying along the beach toward the path which led up to the settlement.

He was seventeen now, tall and browned from his lively outdoor life. In one hand he carried a pair of big, fine-looking sea bass, held by a long strip of beachgrass threaded through their gills. In the other was a half-stripped bunch of grapes and his chin was dripping with the thick tawny juice.

TO GO OR STAY?

Humphrey was pleased with his morning's work. It was a good way to begin any day and the fish would provide a splendid meal for the family. The number who daily gathered around the Dares' board had increased notably in the three years they had lived on Roanoke Island.

It was natural that Humphrey had gone to live with Eleanor and Ananias Dare because their families had been neighbors in Yorkshire. And when Georgie Howe, aged five, was orphaned by the enemy Indian's arrow which had killed his father on the day after their arrival in Roanoke, it was Eleanor who could make room for him because the Dares had the largest house. That was one privilege Ananias had as Chief Patentee, because he was acting governor in his father-in-law's stead.

The young Widow Pierce, who wanted to be useful, proved a splendid housekeeper for Eleanor Dare and became later Virginia's devoted nurse. When Henry Berry, the blacksmith, with an eye for a home and family of his own, asked Jane Pierce to marry him, she refused to leave the new baby. So Henry moved in, too, at the Dares' when the wedding was over.

Humphrey wiped his chin by nudging it against his shirt sleeve and hurried along with his catch. Jane would have some sharp remarks to make about the state of his shirt and he grinned in anticipation.

What would they have done, he wondered now, if John White had returned? He was a stern man and he wouldn't have liked the babies' squalling. The arrival of young William Dare, a most demanding child, two months after Jane's first son, Henry, had been a trial for them all. But babies happened to everybody and no one in the Dare household had died of the double calamity.

When Humphrey rounded a turn in the path, there sat Georgie on a favorite flat stone alongside, waiting for him.

"They want you," he announced, without other greeting, "fast as you can get there. No, it's not because of the fish." The little boy eyed Humphrey's catch critically. "I hope it's enough for all," he said, doubtfully. "Manteo and his mother have come and they'll be eating with us today."

"What's toward?" Humphrey asked.

Manteo and his mother had not been expected, so it must be something special. He handed Georgie the grapes and pulled him up to walk along to the house.

"I couldn't hear all they said," said Georgie, frankly, stuffing in the juicy fruit as fast as he could swallow. "They talked a lot and then Nias said you'd got to call the Patentees for a meeting. This afternoon."

Humphrey groaned. He had had other plans for later in the day. There was never enough time for everything—his duties as a member of the Dare household and as a young colonist, added to all the want-to-do's that island life and his own ambitions stirred in him, after his Latin lessons with the rector, John Brooke, were accomplished each day.

He had sailed with the colonists in the hope that

TO GO OR STAY?

he could create in the New World another manor like the one he had inherited in Yorkshire, and though there hadn't been enough land cleared on Roanoke so far for that realization, he still hoped for it and had set himself to learn many wilderness skills from the friendly Indians nearby so that he would be ready to run his farm when the time came.

The Indians were a tribe of Corees whose extensive forests and farms were on the mainland but they spent a part of each year during the spring-into-summer season especially at their fishing camp on the next island where they dried their heavy catch for winter food.

One of their young men, Manteo, had been taken to the English court by Sir Richard Grenville, who had headed an earlier expedition to the New World and, returning home, Manteo had been given passage on *The Lion*, the ship which brought John White's people to Roanoke. He knew English speech and English manners and the presence of his family at the fishing camp when the ship arrived in that July of three years past had been the colonists' great good fortune, in more than one way.

Humphrey lengthened his stride so that Georgie had to trot to keep up and the child's further attempts to talk came out jerkily. He threw the bare grape stem away and clutched the seam of Humphrey's trousers.

"They did say . . ." pant, pant . . . "something about . . . going away. Humph . . . rey . . . I did hear that. You'll take me . . ." puff, puff . . . "with you, won't you . . . h'm, Humph . . . rey?"

Lady of Roanoke

"I'm not going anywhere, far's I know," said Humphrey, firmly, with only half his mind on the little boy's chatter. "Except running around to the houses to tell the men about the meeting. That'd be no fun, following me about. Besides, somebody must mind the babies when we have company. Hadn't you thought about that, Georgie?"

They had reached the level so Georgie recovered his breath enough to say, scornfully, "Babies! And boy ones, especially that William. He yells if you rock him and yells if you don't. There'll be some women around to see Manteo's mother. They can help with the babies. H'm, Humphrey? Can't I . . . ?"

Humphrey said abruptly, "I've an idea for you. You go call John and Billy for me while I see Nias and find out what I'm to say to the Patentees. The big boys can help call the meeting and then we'll go down to the swimming place and have a wash while the fish cook."

Jane took the fish without a word about Humphrey's shirt. She looked a bit grim so he forebore teasing her.

Manteo and Mary seemed as usual, but Humphrey sensed that their visit was not a casual morning drop-in call. They had come over from the fishing camp for some special purpose.

The fragrance of the grape season was in the house, too. Someone had brought a heap of them in for the meal and they were piled on their own leaves in the center of the big table. The glare of the sun outside, as the morning grew warmer, made the big room seem dark and the grapes were a lovely focus for light. A wandering bee buzzed above them.

Nias said, "Ah, Humphrey, I'm glad Georgie found you. Please go and speak to every Patentee, wherever he is at work in the settlement, and bid him come to the chapel after the mid-day meal to meet me there. We will have a matter to discuss. Pastor Brooke should join us today and you will come in please, and be doorkeeper."

Humphrey felt subdued when he went out again, forgetting the state of his clothing, to find the two big boys of the colony waiting—John Sampson, son of the Patentee, and Billy Wythers, nephew of George Martyn who was not one. They were almost-fourteens, as they themselves described their age, and were practically inseparable.

Evidently Georgie had told them about the prospects for swimming because their faces fell when Humphrey explained what Nias had said.

"I thought if you two helped we'd get through fast and there'd be time for a good dip before the noon meal. Now, from the look of things, I'd better not go. Nias may want something more of me. And I ought to talk to Manteo, too, if I can separate him from Nias. Probably not."

"How long will the meeting last?" John asked. "Could we go afterward?"

Humphrey shook his head. "Who knows?"

"Didn't Nias tell you what it's about?" This from Billy.

"They don't, usually," Humphrey answered, "and today, not an extra word. It must be something pretty special though, with Manteo and Mary arriving when we didn't look for'm to be coming and the call for the meeting right after."

John shrugged. "Might as well help, anyway, Billy," he said. To Humphrey, "Not much going on right now. We plucked a goose for Mistress Harvie this morning. She's saving the feathers for a pillow and it has to be done just so, her plucking. . . . What do we say to the Patentees? Nine of'm to tell, we'll each take three and you do the other two besides Nias, and rector, sir. You'll like to talk to him, anyway, you do it so easy, but then he's your teacher."

"Could be yours, too, if you'd only be willing," Humphrey retorted.

John ignored that and asked, "What, after we tell'm?"

"Nothing, after we eat, except wait and see," said Humphrey.

He turned to Georgie. "You sit right there, on the doorstep and don't move. If anyone comes along you are not to say what John and Billy and I are doing. Don't, above all, tell'm we've got company, though I suppose the whole settlement already knows it. You hear? We'll come back when our work is done."

It was an entirely useless order, he felt, except that it might make Georgie feel important enough to obey and that would take care of his whereabouts for a while.

Though there was nothing to excite anyone in the verbal announcement of the Patentees' meeting to take

place in the early afternoon, the colony was easily
alerted by any unusual thing. Today it seemed almost
as if people had been waiting for something to happen.
It explained the gathering of colonists outside the
chapel when the Patentees began to assemble later,
singly and in twos. Ananias came last and when
Humphrey nodded that all the others were present, he
said, "Come along, then," and stepped inside.

There was an audible murmur from the crowd at
that and Humphrey heard a low-voiced comment,
which was so pointedly aimed at him, that he was in
no hurry to close the door. He pretended to be having
trouble with the latch.

"What's *he* doin' at the Patentees' meeting? All he
knows is Latin. If they're havin' extras in today, why
not pick from those as has done something' for the
colony?"

A brief glance out over the heads of the people
from Humphrey's vantage on the chapel doorstone
wasn't sufficient to locate the speaker, but it had
sounded like Mark Bennet's voice and Mark was there,
standing close.

Humphrey tried not to let on that he had heard,
by calling to John and Billy, "Wait for me?" in the
most natural voice he could manage, and went in and
closed the door.

There was a deep silence inside and Humphrey
felt awed and full of anticipation, which banished his
momentary annoyance that anyone in the colony could
have been so petty. If they didn't know by this time,
they'd better learn that it was only because he lived in

Lady of Roanoke

Nias's house and was handy to run errands that he was present in the meeting today. It was his first time at such a gathering.

How did the Patentees conduct a meeting? Did they have a set pattern the same as ritual in church? His own feeling today was different from that on Sundays.

Nias and the rector sat in the pulpit, facing the men and presently Nias stood up and after the prayer, asked Dion Harvie to call the roll. Dion scarcely looked at his book as he intoned the Patentees' names, purely a formality because they were all there—Dare, Bayly, Cooper, Sampson, Stevens, Prat, Harvie, Nichols, Dimmocke, White. Only one absent, the last read, John White, Governor.

After that there was an audible, collective sigh from all the men, like a lament without words sweeping briefly through the chapel.

It became clear then to Humphrey, waiting alone, set apart at the door, that a crisis was expected. Small sounds came through from outside. The people had sensed it, too. They hadn't gone away.

There was no ritual.

Nias said, bluntly as could be, "Manteo and his mother came this morning with the news that they are going home to the mainland in a few days and they feel strongly that we should go with them, that it is more than wise. They have noted our Governor's long absence and feel with us that it is strange. This group of Corees have stayed on far longer than their custom is, even through last winter, for our sake, as all of you

know. Now the old chief is ailing and word has come
they must return. Another part of the tribe will come
here and take a turn at the fish curing."

The men looked at each other and whispered together before anyone made audible comment or asked
a question. Each was reluctant to be the first.

It was Christopher Cooper, always an impatient
man, who finally got to his feet.

"Can't see the importance," he said. "The Corees
have been friendly from the start. What is the difference which group is our neighbor?"

Roger Bayly was next. "What if we should go and
the Governor not find us? Seems as if he's been gone
long enough, that it'd be any day now for him to return."

Dion Harvie argued about that. "We've never had
any guarantee that all the Corees are our friends.
We've never seen some of them. Perhaps these three
years here have dulled our wits somewhat. Manteo is
only a young chief and I understand they are bound
by tribal laws. If he has been sent for, it is his duty
to go back to the mainland. Those who come to take
the places of these now here may not like us to the
extent that Manteo's family has. I remind you, too, that
we arranged with Governor White for just such a circumstance as this—what we would do if the need arose
to leave this place in his absence. And what we'd do
with his things in the event. You've not forgotten that
paper, surely?"

He sat down, and there were several affirmative
nods.

"But what if he never returns?" Roger Bayly was persistent. "And we, inland. It means we'd be cut off from England . . . as long as . . . for the rest of our natural . . . lives." His voice sank.

Nias said, calmly, "That's the risk we take, Roger. We do have the choice of staying here and becoming Spanish prisoners before the year is out, possibly."

No one could tell from Nias's face how he would vote. He was allowing all sides of the matter to show, if they brought them out, Humphrey saw, and he wondered how he would vote, if he could. It was a solemn thing to decide, for all the people on Roanoke as well as the babe yet unborn to Elizabeth Viccars.

John Nichols got up slowly and he spoke as if he was feeling his way through his thoughts. "There's another responsibility we have, and that's our Patentees' contract with Sir Walter."

Nias said, briskly, "None of the terms have been carried out on either side, John. Think on it. We were to be landed near Chesapeake Bay where we expected to be allotted five hundred acres of land, each . . . and Sir Walter was to receive one-fifth of all the gold we'd find. We've not found any here."

"But the Queen . . ."

"Gave Letters Patent to Sir Walter Raleigh to plant colonies and he acted under that document to contract with us," said Nias, patiently.

"But he still could hold us responsible . . . if he found us . . . couldn't he?" John hung onto his fear.

TO GO OR STAY?

No one answered him and he went on, "If there's any doubt about future Indian friendship here, we'd be foolish not to go with Manteo and Mary. We've done our best on Roanoke though all we've accomplished is to keep alive, so far. We ought to face plain facts . . . our very existence seems to depend on our decision today, without respect to the Patentees' contract with Sir Walter. As personal investment, I think that's lost."

It was the most outspoken of any speech yet made, and the men sat silent, thinking of it.

The sounds outside were growing louder when Chris Cooper sprang up, again.

"Seems to me," he said, "that we could argue all afternoon and not get any forrader. We haven't the right to make all the decision in this matter . . . the people are out there, Nias. Bid them come in and let's talk together. The women aren't used to speaking in public, it's true, but their husbands'll know how they feel about things. They can tell. Let's have a colony meeting."

Nias asked for a vote on that and all hands went up.

He had meant to have one, Humphrey was sure, else he'd have sent the people away in the beginning.

Nias came down off the pulpit and asked Humphrey to open the door, quite formally. When he stood on the stone and bade the people come in, those in front scarcely let him step aside before they surged through, so great was their anxiety. They went as habit led to the seats they usually occupied on Sunday, the men on one side and the women on the other. They hadn't brought the children in.

That was a mistake, Humphrey thought, but the babies' crying would have disturbed the meeting. His mouth quivered with a smile he couldn't allow to appear. Was Georgie at home, minding William Dare and Henry Berry? And where was Virginia, the little mischief?

When he had complete silence, Nias asked the rector to say a prayer again as was his custom to do when all came together for any reason. Then he rose in the pulpit and explained once more about the invitation from Manteo and Mary—no one could pronounce her Indian name so the women had given her an English one—and said that though the Patentees had discussed it, they did not want to decide alone about a matter that would affect everyone there.

He said, "The question is, *Shall we go or stay?*"

He talked a long time and the people listened patiently while he presented the case, as a pleader might in a court, Humphrey thought, a summary of what the Patentees had said and he to them, earlier.

"If we go inland, there will be packing to attend to. Manteo is willing to wait a reasonable time for that. We discussed many details with him and his mother this morning. If we remain here, Manteo says there will be need of extra fortification, and more provision of dried and cured food to be laid by for the winter."

Some of the housewives nodded at each other, approving that, and others frowned thoughtfully.

TO GO OR STAY?

"If you vote to stay here, the risk is not entirely that the new group of Coree Indians may not be friendly, or that the other tribes, now apparently peaceful, may rise up again. Another matter has been growing daily more clear—that something very dire must have happened to our Governor, else he'd surely have returned to us before now. Until the Spanish caravel appeared recently and was so mysteriously blown up, which saved us all from being made prisoners, I doubt not, we have not seen the sail of any other country since our good ship *The Lion* went back to England. Have you thought on't?"

The question brought a little murmur of response, before he went on.

"We have been living in a fool's Paradise somewhat, and on the bounty of our Indian friends, albeit we have improved our physical comfort of late in the houses and with increased crop yield. Now, friends, how do you say? We must decide this question today, now, here in our chapel. We will stay until the *going down of the sun* if need be, because, if the decision is to go inland, we'll have so little time for the thought and preparation necessary for such a trip. I dare not lessen the importance of your decision at that point. After the boats from Manteo's camp ferry us across, we'll have to *walk* and carry loads."

Anthony Cage was the first colonist to speak. He had never been one, in the true sense, was rather an out-and-out adventurer and he had been one of the chief grumblers because they hadn't found gold.

"Speakin' for myself," he said, "I'm for leavin' here, no matter how the rest of you decide. We haven't found what we came for—what I came for—and that's gold. Spose'n Sir Walter gets impatient and sends a ship along to collect? He could hold the colony responsible, couldn't he, for a return on all the outfittin' of the expedition? And who of us has the money to pay?" He sat down with a sour grin on his face.

"That is to say," Dion Harvie answered him, with a nod to Nias for permission, "you feel we have some debt to Sir Walter? But we can't do the impossible. He didn't expect that. If he was led to think that gold existed where it plainly doesn't, that wasn't our fault. And remember, we are not living where we had expected to."

"They said gold was all over," Anthony Cage retorted.

Charles Florrie, Cage's bunk mate, rose then and made his own declaration. "I been waitin' for this chance. Knew it would come. I'm askin' plain and open that you give me and all who want to go with me, our share of the present supplies, and we'll take ourselves off your hands tomorrow and go along down the coast. We ain't so certain some gold hasn't been picked up here and not reported. What gold I find, later, will all be mine, an I escape Indians *and* Spanish as well as bein' rid of a colonist's worries. That's my say and no thanks due Sir Walter Raleigh."

"And mine, and mine, and mine," a chorus followed, a good half of the single men in the colony.

Nias was equal to the unexpected direction the

thinking had taken. "Then I must say," he answered suavely, "that none of you can have further interest in our deliberations. We will excuse you now and if this company votes as you ask, we will set you on your way tomorrow."

They were a little surprised at such speedy acceptance of their defiance, that was plain, but they put on a mien of gay bravado and went swaggering out of chapel, boisterously talking of the riches they meant to find and keep for themselves.

The startled colonists were relieved on the whole to have the true nature of the men so oddly revealed, though it had always been hard to get them to do their share of any work. Now all was clear.

Nias rapped for order which the incident had disturbed. He said, "Gentlemen . . . ah . . . and ladies . . . I must remind you that our immediate concern is the safety of our families and the expediency of hiding in the wilderness from marauding shipping, if the English sails do not appear."

He was completely ignoring the idea that Sir Walter Raleigh would present a bill for payment.

"We are offered protection and the use of land to cultivate for food if we remove from this place with our friends, the Corees. Shall we accept? Go, or stay? How do you say?"

Ambrose Viccars was on his feet, immediately. "Nias, can we adjourn, right in here, and talk to our wives? And then come to order again? We've never had a precedent for such a decision as Manteo offers us and . . ."

Lady of Roanoke

"Hear, hear," came again.

And so it was agreed. When they reassembled, more formally, the worried look had changed to one of resolve on so many faces that Humphrey thought, "We're going" and his heart gave a queer, exultant leap. He felt guilty to be glad. But now, he might yet find room to build his manor, have his own farm, and plant crops that would yield food for the whole colony.

He forgot about John White's destiny and Spanish caravels that might come. The long walk across fifty miles of forest trails didn't daunt him. And he was not surprised at the vote.

It was unanimous acceptance of the Corees' invitation to go with them in two days' time across the Sound and begin that inland journey.

It was four o'clock when the meeting ended, as afterward noted by Pastor Brooke in his diary.

Outside, in a patient group, were John and Billy, all the children and Lion, Humphrey's dog. Georgie hadn't stayed home to mind the babies. The big boys had carried the Dares' cradle to the chapel yard and in it lay Henry and William, placidly asleep, with Lion on guard. Virginia was doing her best to wake them up by standing on the back rocker, where she was hidden by the hood when Billy's eye strayed. The little minx.

Georgie's shrill, reproachful voice echoed above the other little boys', who were begging Humphrey to take them swimming.

"Humphrey, why did you stay in there so long? What were all the people doing? Do we have to take

all these down to our pool? You said I could go, and
John and Billy . . ."

Over the little boy's blond head, Humphrey met
the big boys' amused eyes. He said apologetically,
"We'll have to take'm all. There's so little time left
before we leave, for them to enjoy it."

"Leave?" said John. "Where's who going?"

"I told you," Georgie yelled. "Manteo said . . ."
and then he stopped and covered his mouth with his
hand and looked in awe at Humphrey's accusing grin.

"And *I* told *you* not to talk," said Humphrey.

He smiled at the almost-fourteens. "All of us," he
explained, "are going to the mainland with Manteo's
folks, in two days' time. Come along, shift the cradle
back to the house and let the women look after those
young'uns and Virginia. We'll have our swim."

"But I want to come, too," Virginia wailed.

"No, little Lady, not this time. This is a boys'
party, strictly."

She thumped the hard ground with her small, im-
perious foot. "I shall go. My mother said . . ."

"Nothing about swimming," said Eleanor, ap-
proaching. "Go along, Humphrey, I'll see to her."

The boys lifted the cradle, carefully, and the sleeping infants—six and eight months old in an uncertain
world—did not stir. They were used to noise.

The six little boys of the colony trailed after, not
fully understanding the import of what Humphrey had
said to Billy and John, though the magic word *swim*
was fully clear.

PREPARATION

2

Manteo and his mother hadn't been able to wait to hear the result of the colonists' meeting, so Manteo returned early the next morning to find out what they had decided.

He arrived in time to witness the departure of the men who were determined to leave Roanoke and continue their search for gold which had been completely unrewarding so far.

Most of the people showed their good manners and greater good will by going down to the shore to watch them set out, southward, crowded into one of the Indian-style long log boats. Ananias had been generous

PREPARATION

in handing out the share of supplies they asked for, but it seemed they couldn't get away fast enough, for fear the colonists might change their minds at the last.

It was observed that they could produce a boat made by themselves when the need for it arrived. Manteo had not given it to them.

Humphrey looked on with mixed feelings. Until yesterday he had forgotten the stipulation in the Patentees' grant from Sir Walter that he should have five percent of whatever gold they found. They had lived long enough on Roanoke to realize one did not pick up nuggets of it, lying about on the ground like windfall apples. There might be gold somewhere in the New World, else expeditions wouldn't have been sent to find it, but there wasn't any hereabouts. That they knew now, too truly.

Gold, for most of the colonists, when they thought about it at all, had become the color of ripe corn after a good harvest, or a woman's blonde head, bowed at table for a blessing on the meal she had cooked for her family. It was also the tint in gloriously awesome sunsets after a good day's work was done. Humphrey wondered if they'd see as lovely ones inland, as they had here in the open above the ocean.

When the log boat was out of sight the people turned back, up the beach path to the settlement to begin preparations for their own departure.

Henry Berry shook his head in pity. "Give'm three months, mayhap less, to starve to death," he said, mournfully. "Every one of'm hates to work. Surprised me, it did, when they brought out that boat. They could spend time on theirsels, right enough. Gold's all they think about, else, only reason they came with us. I wish'm joy of all they scratch up. First Spanish ship that comes'll relieve'm of it, find they any."

His wife said, "Worryin' won't feed their like, did they rate your feelin's, Henry. Seems we're well rid."

The women held their own meeting at the Dares' house that morning to talk over the move which their menfolk had voted for. They had plenty to say among themselves, away from the chapel, when they began planning the break-up of their first home in the New World. Everything was precious, but was it sensible to burden themselves with heavy loads?

"We should take all of everything that's movable," said Margery Harvie, firmly. "I'll want to take my geese."

"And we, our cows," Elizabeth Viccars added.

"Even if the birds and beasts slow us on the trail, we'll be with friends all the way," Joan Warner reminded them. "Manteo's people take everything when they go back and forth. So can we. Somebody should have spoken of this yesterday in the chapel."

"You mean one of us women?" Margery asked, incredulously. "Not but what I think we'll get our say out loud, one of these days. I couldn't believe what I was hearing, Elizabeth, when your Ambrose asked to have an adjournment so he could talk to you. He practically admitted in public that he depends on your judgment."

"Could have had our say out loud, then and there,

had we held out for it," said Jane Berry. "But it's best not to push things. Except for a big matter like this, I don't mind Henry decidin' for both of us." She chuckled. "He thinks he does, anyway, forgettin' my opinion on whatever 'tis given out the day before or at breakfast."

Humphrey heard a good deal of what they said at their meeting because of an order from Nias. He and John and Billy were to stay within call and help the women in any way they could—run errands, pack, mind the babies, whatever was asked of them. The men were taking advantage of the two days' time to make some rough supply-carriers for the journey.

It was a long day and a great relief when Eleanor dismissed the three lads and they were free to run down for another cooling swim in the pool Humphrey had discovered shortly after their arrival on Roanoke. It lay beneath a cliff, protected from wind, and though landlocked was cleared and filled again daily by the outrushing and inrushing tides.

He was thoughtful as they went down the path. He was seeing more of the two almost-fourteens in these exciting past few hours than he had for weeks at a time before. The more than three years difference in their ages had been partly responsible. The rest was the others' complete indifference to schooling.

They paddled and splashed and dived like young porpoises, and when their spirits were restored they lay awhile on the sand in the remaining warmth of the lowering sun and talked.

"What's the good of all your Latin now?" John demanded.

"It's good for my mind," said Humphrey, almost automatically. He'd had to endure the same observations from several of the grownups about the time spent on his study.

"All I meant, Humphrey," John pursued, "if we'd had any chance of going back to England, you might have made some use of it, you being a gentleman's son and all, but now . . ."

"I think we should forget about who we were," said Humphrey, abruptly. "We've been doing everything together here, haven't we?"

"So we have!" said Billy. "I never thought about it before. Think you, h'm, we'll ever see England again?"

"Do you want to?" Humphrey asked, "And why worry about it now?"

"No need," said Billy. "I was just asking, after I heard . . ." he hesitated.

"Out with it, then. Probably you'll feel better," Humphrey urged.

"Some of the colonists think the same as those who left this morning . . . afraid we might have to pay something back to Sir Walter on the cost of this expedition, specially that we haven't found any gold."

Humphrey said, "Nonsense. Sir Walter is an honorable man. They discussed the whole thing in Patentees' meeting before the colonists were invited in. He wouldn't be that unreasonable."

PREPARATION

"That's what my father said," John Sampson broke in.

"My uncle George said it, too," Billy hastened to assure them, "but it does look as if some voted to leave, so they'd escape any payment that might come due."

"Pure nonsense, more of it. Governor White will find us when he returns and then, of course, Sir Walter will know, so if anyone voted to go to the mainland for the sake of escape, they'll be fooled. I look on it as a chance to live better while we are waiting for the Governor to come. Don't you?"

"Just going with our folks," said John. "My father and his uncle, eh, Billy?"

"Only reason," said Billy.

Humphrey was glad that the talk presently veered to hunger and the coming meal. Lads like these shouldn't be worried with grownups' motives for decisions they made. Billy and John must be bothered a little by the recent talk or they wouldn't have asked any questions. He had one or two of his own. Might it not be that some of the colonists had other reasons for voting as they did, which hadn't come out in the arguments? So might the blusterers who had departed that morning.

John and Billy needed work to do, and that was coming if the signs weren't all wrong. Humphrey's anticipation returned. Somewhere beyond the Sound, in the depths of the Corees' forest lands, was lying the particular piece that would one day be his . . . a manor of his own creation and cultivation. He hadn't chosen a name for it yet, but that would come.

Lady of Roanoke

The next morning Eleanor looked at the cradle dubiously. "It's so heavy," she said to Humphrey, who was the only other member of the family then present, "I wonder if . . ."

Humphrey asked, anxiously, "You wouldn't think of leaving it here, would you? I can carry it on my back."

"Such a young back, for so heavy a burden." She was still dubious.

Humphrey grinned. "But strong. Look at my muscle. My garden and the rowing to Manteo's camp . . . and looking after my heifer . . ." His face clouded. "I forgot about her. If I carry the cradle . . ."

"Your little cow can be herded along with Ambrose Viccars' . . ." said Ananias, "if I heard it right," as he came in. "Come, Eleanor, the women want you to help decide . . ."

She turned to follow him out and the rest of the women's need was lost to Humphrey. There was a great deal to discuss and plan in too short a time.

But it was settled in his own mind that the cradle would go with them. It would be a shame to leave it. Three years before he had carried it ashore when the colonists left *The Lion* and landed on Roanoke. The little rocking bed was sturdily built and would last many a generation of children.

It was the last thing to be carried down to the shore, when they left the following morning. Humphrey ran back for it when all his other responsibilities were seen to, and he stood for a moment in the dismantled room.

PREPARATION

Jane Berry had left it swept and neat from long habit, but the whole place looked forlorn in the early light. It had been a lively household and Humphrey wondered if they'd experience its like ever again. Everything would probably be different in the new settlement they'd make, somewhere in the mainland greenwood.

How long would it take for the vines to grow in through the casement openings and the deer to find there was again shelter for them in these deserted rooms? That had been the condition of all the houses—signs of animal occupancy—and thick vines covering all the windows—when they had arrived three years past.

It was too gloomy a thought for such a lovely morning.

He stooped, pulled a heavy strap through the braces of the rockers and got the cradle onto his back, with the rim of the hood resting on a pad across his forehead as he had seen the Indians adjust heavy packs.

And then he was away, down the beach path for the last time, without a backward look.

EVENING

3

It took a long time to ferry so many people and their goods across the Sound in Manteo's boats, but when it was done, there was nothing on the seaward side to show that the vines and trailing willow branches, where they entered the forest, had ever been disturbed. On the landward side low bushes hid the boats safely, for the Indians' use on another trip.

Mary led the line-up—the married people and their families, the staunch single men and widowers and the three spinsters, and Manteo's people as escort—with two of her little Barbary ponies, tamed from wild herds on the islands.

Everybody carried something, even down to Little Amby Viccars. He was such a small fellow to be carrying anything, but the basket of grapes he started out with would be empty in a few hours. He was also supposed to keep one sassy Harvie gander in order, all the way from Roanoke to wherever they would one day make a second home. Its wings had been clipped. It couldn't stray far.

Everyone who thought about it at all knew they'd have a slow and tedious progress because of their many possessions. So they were pleasantly surprised at the fair distance they made that first day when they finally stopped to prepare a hot meal and camp for the night. Supper and sleep under a greenwood tree was nothing new for any colonist, but good food and a long rest were necessary to make ready for the morrow's demands on courage and bodies alike.

Humphrey volunteered to stir the stew after the fire had been laid and the huge iron pot was slung above the flames. He discarded his deerskin jacket and shirt on a bush before he grasped the big wooden paddle and began to stir the food.

The heavy silver ring with the amethyst stone which he wore on a chain around his neck, glinted in the firelight. It was the one treasure besides his birthday gold sovereigns that he had brought from England.

Ananias sat on a log nearby with Virginia on his knee. The little girl was yawning deeply, at shorter and shorter intervals.

"Ah no, little Lady," Humphrey coaxed, "don't

go to sleep now. Supper is almost ready. Aren't you hungry, little maid?"

She stirred and sat straighter within her father's arms, fighting sleep. "I will be hungry, Humphrey, if *you* fill my bowl and feed me out of it. Now that we have William, my mother doesn't . . ."

The end of her sentence was lost in her father's great shout of laughter. He winked at Humphrey.

"Master William in her cradle, though she is too big for it now, has somewhat put our little Lady of Roanoke out of countenance," he said. "I had suspected it, but this is first proof."

It had been there to see, Humphrey thought, but Nias had been too worried of late to notice much that wasn't pointed out to him unless it had to do with the colony's needs. It was good to hear him laugh.

Humphrey leaned to the fire and covered the leaping flame to moderate the heat and drops of sweat from his forehead sizzled on the coals. It was warm work, this, but he daren't spoil the first hot meal they had stopped to prepare since leaving Roanoke at dawn.

Virginia slipped from her father's knee and came to Humphrey, leaning against him as he half knelt after tending the fire. He reached up for the paddle and went on slowly stirring the food while he absently smoothed the tumbled curls around the edge of the little girl's muslin cap and then put his arm around the small figure. She looked like a miniature woman in her long dress, but it wouldn't be any time before she, too, would be in deerskin unless there were still plenty of Eleanor's dresses in her chests to make over.

EVENING

Though Virginia was Humphrey's godchild, she was also the only sister he'd ever have, and he had tended her like one from birth on Roanoke, alternately with teasing when she got old enough to know what it meant. It was fun to see the sparks flash in her lovely eyes and watch the tiny foot in a clumsy homemade shoe beat the ground when she was in a temper. Young Virginia Dare had much spirit.

Humphrey sighed and came out of daydreaming about Roanoke to find that Virginia had gone to sleep standing up against him. He hadn't realized she had stopped talking.

Poor little maid! What should he do? He let the paddle go and called to Margery Harvie to come and serve the meal. It must be cooked by this time. That roused Virginia and she declared stoutly, between more wide yawns, that she now had a mort of hunger and why was he, Humphrey, so slow with his work?

When the bowls had been filled with the stew and some filled again, John Brooke rose in his place and the glow from the fire lighted his serene countenance as he began the familiar words of *Evensong*. The text he chose for the lesson wasn't the one for that day as prescribed in the prayer book, but it was perfect for the colonists.

And the evening and morning were the first day, he read, sounding deeply moved.

This was the twilight of their first day in a hoped-for Eden, or a Promised Land. Like Abraham, though they had left Roanoke to roam *not knowing whither,* not definitely at least, each knew that in God's good time they would come to that place, which, without consciously giving it a description, had different dimensions and held various hopes for each grownup there. Not all wanted a manor with filled barns as Humphrey dreamed of his new Gilling.

Humphrey had a strong feeling that he would know, without any doubt, would recognize the perfect spot for him when they reached it. Somewhere in the woods ahead of them, three days journey, a week, a month—when the time came, he would know it.

So the morning and the evening melted into night and the colonists slept in camp with only their appointed guards awake, as the hours went by and each stood his watch in turn.

Humphrey was one, clad in shirt and deerskin jacket once more because Eleanor felt it proper, and with his dog Lion at his knee. He was proud that Nias Dare had chosen him to stand with the men. He was as tall as any and he could top Ambrose Viccars a few inches.

He stared out into the darkness all about, no stars visible because the leaves were so thick on the trees, and wondered what was ahead of them all, older and younger, out there beyond the ring of light from the flickering campfire, along the way they would travel tomorrow?

LONG WALK

4

It was not yet light next morning so that the Harvie geese hadn't announced the new day, when the camp began to stir. The few voiced complaints were subdued. The colonists were hardened now to crowding, to communal life, to lack.

Here they were, not all of them fully assured, even yet, that it was the right thing to do, but doing it because the majority thought it was, starting out at the time-of-the-paling-of-the-stars, as the Indians said, without breakfast. That would come later when they stopped for a rest.

Humphrey sighed and longed for a dip in the pool

Lady of Roanoke

under the cliff at Roanoke. He hoped the pleasant land he dreamed of would be near good springs.

He sat on the pallet of Spanish moss where he had slept briefly when his turn at guard was done, yawning and lazily scratching Lion between his ears, while he tried to decide if it was useless to find Manteo and ask if he knew of a pool or spring hereabout.

And then he saw Georgie beckoning anxiously and forgot about clean water for washing his face. He hastily buttoned his shirt and smoothed his hair, called Lion to heel and followed the child, stepping over some late sleepers on the way.

Georgie led him to the spot under a sheltering tree where the cradle still stood as he had seen it the night before. Evidently this was the place where the whole Dare family had spent the night. Now young William lay placidly sleeping still and Virginia stood by, glowering.

Humphrey raised an eyebrow at Eleanor and whispered, "Trouble?" and she nodded.

Virginia said, "My feet hurt, Humphrey."

"Did you get a stone in your shoe? Put your foot up and let me see." He knelt down, ready to oblige.

"I can't put both up at once, Humphrey Hall. I'd fall down if I did. I don't want to fall down. I want to ride."

He said, gravely, while almost choking to keep his face calm and hold laughter in, "And where did you think of riding?"

"In my cradle."

"But William is in it, and you are getting so tall that . . ."

"I can sit in it, if William isn't in the way."

"How did you come yesterday, from the island to this place?"

"My father carried me on his shoulder and my mother carried William and . . ."

"And I carried the cradle," said Humphrey, not letting her finish, "and I'm not going to carry it today with you in it. You'd fall out." He let the laughter come, a very funny thing—Virginia falling out of her cradle—and she laughed, too.

"Somebody else can take it today and I'll ride on your shoulder, Humphrey," she said with a speculating, wide-eyed glance upward.

Humphrey stood up, to speak to Eleanor, with his back turned on the stubborn child. "That's probably what was her intent to start with, but you can't carry that heavy baby a second day. Mayhap our little Lady of Roanoke would go with Mary, ride one of the ponies?"

"Something different and strange might help. I didn't think our little maid's temper would show so quickly."

"She's tired like all the rest of the women. I'll take her to Mary and see what might be. And I'll walk with you and carry William."

Mary was delighted but Virginia's nose was still slightly askew when it developed that Mistress Harvie had decided she wanted the geese kept together and

Lady of Roanoke

Little Amby was promoted to the other pony's back. Mary walked between the small horses and held the children on in front of her loads of dried fish and so, once more, the strange cavalcade started on another day's journey toward their new home.

Humphrey saw Mark Bennet shoulder the one spinning wheel they had brought. It belonged to Mistress Tappan. Audrey was a generous woman and it would spin all day long, had they wool. If the Corees had sheep, perhaps Virginia wouldn't have to wear deerskin. But how could the spun thread be made into cloth?

An astonishing wave of discouragement swept over Humphrey's usually buoyant spirit with the question, as he hurried back to the end of the line where Eleanor waited. If only John White had returned, as he promised, with needed goods, then the women wouldn't be worried with the contriving he had seen them working at so busily in recent months. What was the use of it, anyway? It would have been better for all if they had returned home with Governor White.

Humphrey couldn't know that part of his feeling of futility was physical hunger, nor that he was scowling ferociously when he took the baby from Eleanor and grasped an end of the cradle which she signed for them to carry together. It was clumsy going and he knew when they started that they couldn't travel far in such fashion. The Berry brothers must be finding Henry's anvil equally awkward, and much heavier.

It was the first time Humphrey had been alone with Eleanor, to have any conversation with her, since the morning they had discussed bringing the cradle along. She had always been willing to listen to him, from as far back as he could remember, had encouraged him to break away from his Uncle Jeremy's distasteful plans for his future—no farms for Humphrey in those—and come with the colonists. From the first moment he had spoken of it on a long gone Sunday afternoon in Yorkshire she had said it was the right thing for him.

"The Corees will have to set aside a lot of land, seems to me," he remarked, as they struggled along with the cradle and William, "if each family is to have some."

"Oh, no, Humphrey, that's not the way it will be at all. Oh, I do wish you had been with us when Mary and Manteo came the other day. They assumed then that we will go on living in the same way we have on Roanoke—produce our food in common and provide for each other—crops, anyway. That's all it will be."

"But Eleanor, how may I then . . .?"

"Oh, your manor!" she broke in. "Hasn't Nias told you? He mentioned your fair hope to Manteo and he got that gleam in his eye that means humor with him and said he had a plan for you and he was sure you would one day have your farm. But, of course, Humphrey, you'll have to be contented at first to continue as you've been doing on Roanoke—corn between tree stumps, perhaps, and share what you grow . . ."

"That's all right then. I wanted to know." He sighed gustily and added, "Seems we'll be starting all over again . . . if we stay inland . . . Governor White's return might make things different . . . d'you think anyone will want to go back to England when he comes?"

"I don't know, Humphrey."

She didn't enlarge upon her answer and Humphrey looked at her curiously. Then he remembered something he had been wanting to ask about ever since the meeting.

"Eleanor, what did Dion Harvie mean when he said, in the Patentees' meeting, before the rest of you came in, something about an arrangement with your father, and his things? I knew about the sign we'd leave behind, but he mentioned a paper."

"Have you not noticed that his boxes are not in our carrying?"

"No, Eleanor, no, I haven't. Other things to think about. What did you do with them?"

"We buried everything in what we thought a safe place, after dark, the night before we left. That was what the paper was about. An agreement between him and the Patentees. I think he was more concerned about what might chance his books and paints and drawing pencils than how the colony would fare, when he went back to England. The Patentees gave him their bond, which ran somewhat in this way . . ." she stopped and Humphrey was obliged to, too, so he shifted William to a more comfortable position. The movement woke the baby and he howled for his mother.

The cradle was returned to Humphrey's back and Eleanor held her son and tried to hush his cries while she repeated falteringly the words of the promise given

to John White by the Patentees, their bond, in effect—
*that if any part be spoiled or lost, we will see it restored
to you or your assignees whensoever the same shall be
missed and demanded.*

"To make it stronger, they told him, an we were
not there at the time of his return, he was to know we
had departed inland some fifty miles, for the further
safety of all."

"Is it known only to the Patentees, the bond about
the Governor's boxes?"

"Yes, fairly secret. I suppose Margery Harvie
knows, as I do. And now, you."

"And if he comes? This is a big forest to search in."

"You forget Manteo's people. Some of them would
know how to direct him. But it has been so long since
my father left . . . and quite a number welcomed the
chance to . . . seem to disappear, inland . . ."

"Then all the reasons did not come out in the voting. I had a feeling they didn't . . ."

"No, not all. It was thought best . . . I shouldn't
be telling you these things, Humphrey."

"Yes, you should. I'm a part of the colony. We may
never get those blankets and axes and new clothes that
we have needed so desperately at times, since he left."

"But we have seen how the Indians live, from the
land and the sea, and we have you, our good farmer, to
help us. Our coming to the New World has been served,
Humphrey. We have proved there is no gold on Roanoke—have had no way of telling if there is any in the
Chesapeake Bay region—which was Sir Walter's chief

Lady of Roanoke

aim in outfitting us, along with the idea that we spread the Christian faith. That began with Manteo's christening sacrament. It has cost Sir Walter dear, no doubt, and us the more, now that we cannot, an we would, return to our homes in England again. Most of the Patentees would have nothing to go back to, Humphrey, have you thought of that? They invested most of what they owned in the project—they risked not finding gold, too. Some of it was to be theirs. But there will be no dullness here, Humphrey, with plenty of work to do and . . . and . . . the children."

"Yes," he said, "I've been thinking of them, too."

They trudged on silently until Mary signaled, and the line stopped and broke. The ponies whinnied and there was a confused sound of voices and dogs barking. Then the Harvie geese began to honk with all their power.

Humphrey went up on tiptoe, trying to see what had happened. Then he set the cradle down, said, "Breakfast stop, I think," nodded to Eleanor and rushed away.

Eleanor laid William in the cradle and flexed her aching arm.

They had come to a small Indian village, where they were expected, it seemed, because a feast of the fruits of summer had been prepared, fresh green corn, roasted ducks, strawberries heaped on wooden plates. Nias was enjoying the exclamations of surprise. Only he and Manteo and Mary had known, ahead of the others.

Georgie Howe had Lion by the collar, and the dog was straining to get away and join the village protectors, but he sat down obediently, though whimpering deep in his throat when Humphrey spoke his name, sternly.

Virginia came off the pony willingly. She was hot and she had been crying. There was dust in the tear streaks and her curls were tangled. She had done the best she could to get some kind of care and it hadn't been enough. Humphrey rubbed her back while he considered. Georgie's face was dirty, too.

If there was water about, it would be a good idea to dip both children, adding Little Amby as a neighborly gesture and let Lion have a good plunge at the same time. There was Johnnie Prat, too, who had no mother, and a feckless father if ever there was one. Johnnie was usually on the edge of things, a small, wistful observer. Maybe young Master Howe could take on a little responsibility there. He was two years older than Johnnie.

Mary saw Humphrey with the growing knot of children around him and knowing his ways on Roanoke, she guessed his need and beckoned.

"Save us some duck, please, Mary?" he urged, when she led them toward a clump of trees and beyond it was a little stream only a few feet away, chattering over shallow rapids below a clear pool.

The little boys were sent to bring a clean dress for Virginia and while they were gone Humphrey used the soap bark supplied by Mary, with sparkling results. The small bone comb he carried in his deerskin pocket smoothed her curls and the little Lady of Roanoke emerged in good temper once more, with her soiled frock washed and spread on the nearest bush to dry.

They didn't need gold in the wilderness half as much as water and soap and good food, Humphrey reflected. He was still a little stunned by Eleanor's frank admission that all had agreed to deliberately cut themselves off from England. But when he had washed away his own accumulation of trail dust and weariness he came out of the pool with renewed zest. How could his uncle Jeremy possibly find him now?

Afterward, again on the march he wondered for an uncounted time, how much farther they must go, until something in the shape of a tree or the look of a hill, the gleam of water, indeed the sum of them, would say to him, "Begin here, Farmer, you have come home."

When?

Meantime he noted with a peaceful grin that Little Amby was trudging once more, carrying his basket filled now with berries under cool leaves for their supper.

HUMPHREY'S MANOR

5

They walked ten days more and rested many times before the tree and the hill and the stream spoke together in welcome, but not to Humphrey Hall alone.

The trail had been climbing steadily and on a late afternoon it curved to the right, and the weary, trudging people came up onto high rolling ground with trees and grass looking much like the park land surrounding an English country house.

Humphrey set the cradle down, feeling that it must be a dream, and drew away from the others. He didn't want to talk to anyone at that moment. His throat felt tight.

Lady of Roanoke

There were little white flowers, like stars, in the grass, close cropped, he saw, by the Corees' sheep—they did have a flock—and the air was cool and spiced with the fragrance of fresh-cut pine. He drew in a deep lungful of it while he stood at the top of a slope that fell away gently to a narrow valley where a stream rippled. Across it there were hills rising like steps, deeply blue in the distance, with leagues of seemingly unbroken forest on their rounded sides.

He lingered there, feeling free and relaxed for the first time since he took his place in the boat when his turn came to be ferried across the Sound. His whole body responded when he drew in another deep breath and he knew, with that inner vision he was beginning to trust a little, that even if this spot had not been the place Manteo intended them to find, he'd have known it, out of all the pleasant vistas they had seen, as the chosen site for his new Gilling. He had truly come home.

But habit was strong, and he knew there were things he should be doing . . . helping Eleanor or Nias . . . Georgie had had his instructions about Johnnie Prat's needs, long since. He hoped now that the two little boys were looking after Lion.

He turned his back on hills and valley and saw smoke lifting lazily on his left . . . evening fires at the Indian village, probably. From Manteo's description that was the direction it should lie. And then the reason for the deep scent of pine in the air became clear. On the opposite side of the vast park land, piles of freshly felled

trees lay ready to be cut into proper lengths, an anyone, some forlorn colonists, to be exact, might have need
of houses.

The trimmed-off branches were arranged separately,
drying no doubt for future hearth fires. The work of
Manteo's people, Humphrey thought, gratefully, warned
by the same runner or a companion, who had gone
ahead of them to plan that wonderful feast enjoyed on
their second day of marching.

It was evidence that the Indians had used their
precious edged tools—hoarded these twenty years, they
said, from an old shipwreck in the Sound—to make
speedier preparation for the coming of the colonists.
Their usual procedure was to burn a tree at the roots
to fell it, leaving no stump. Here, several dotted the
parkland.

Ah, there was Nias, walking alone toward the
cleared space where the new-cut trees lay. Humphrey
hurried to join him, hoping for direction. What must
they do first, here?

He was panting a little when he arrived and before
he could ask his question Mark Bennet appeared from
behind the highest pile of timber. The carpenter was
sniffing at handfuls of chips and frightening away the
squirrels foraging in the soft litter all about.

"Lots of good hickory and walnut and oak in this,"
he said, without greeting. He spread his hands, measuring and gesturing around the park land. "Nias, I been
thinkin' it'd be a good idea for the whole company to
eat together for a while. Maybe all the time. The houses

could be smaller, so. The less buildin' the better, say I."

Of course he, as master carpenter, would have to see to all the putting together, but he was taking a great deal on himself to talk so, Humphrey thought. There hadn't been any mention of future plans on the trail, that he himself had heard. And at night everyone had been too tired to sit by the fire and discuss building houses. He looked at Nias anxiously, but the feeling lasted only a minute, because he was reassured by a quick turn of his friend's hand. Nias was letting Mark talk but he wasn't calling a fellow Patentee to listen, nor indeed any other colonist from groups nearby.

Mark lifted a sapling pole and squinted along it, importantly. "Might make two dwellings from four walls," he went on, though somewhat tentatively, perhaps expecting objection from Nias, who did not comment. "Divided by an inner one, of course, mud-plastered, same as on Roanoke."

Nias asked, mildly, "And what about a meeting place, have you decided that?"

Humphrey had to pretend to sneeze to hold back laughter, when Mark missed the sarcasm in the question.

He said, "Oh, that's what I meant by all eatin' together. One place for a commons, like. Chapel, dining room, and . . . and the Patentees could use it too."

Very grand and gracious of him, Humphrey thought.

"And the school?"

"School? Didn't have one on Roanoke."

"The rector will insist on it here."

"H'm. Commons, too, s'pose, less'n in one of the dwellings."

"Whose?"

Humphrey thought Mark was about to say, "Yours," but caught the word back in time and said, instead, "Ain't for me to say, is't?"

He had said plenty, already, and knew that Nias was not pleased, without it being expressed, because he didn't answer.

They were turning away, when Mark said, bluntly, looking at Humphrey, "Don't know what we'll do with a fellow like you, in the housing. Not a child, nor yet grown. Oh, not but what there'll be a pallet for you, lad. Come this far, with courage and all, you'll be counted. But livin' can't hap in Roanoke fashion here. Houses there were already built. Here we got to do all new."

"Oh, you needn't worry about me," said Humphrey, confidently. "I mean to have my own place. You've heard me say it, over and over. Every colonist knows. I shan't be a trouble to anyone except for food, which I'll help raise. That's why I'd vote, an I could, for a common table, at first, anyway."

Mark laughed, wryly. "Listen to the young cock crow. Of course you'll help raise the crop. But don't think, because of that bit you did on Roanoke that you know enough to have a place of your own. It's . . . it's . . ." he couldn't finish, he was so scornful.

"But I've got a book," said Humphrey sturdily, puzzled by Mark's antagonism. "I brought it from

England . . . once when I was taken to see the Minster at York, I got it in an old shop. It's by Master Thomas Tusser and it's called *Five Hundred Points of Good Husbandry*. 'Twas published the year I was born. It's a good book."

"For England, maybe," Mark conceded, "but I don't hold with books. This is where you've got to know what you know, right here." He tapped his head.

He turned to Nias, fully expecting agreement, but the Patentee said, only, "Let it be for now, Bennet. There are many decisions ahead. See, yonder, some in the making, I doubt not, that'll be told us later."

He gestured toward the women, who stood together a little way off, talking earnestly and paying no attention to the children, who were running about in a mad game, showing their joyful release from the discipline of the trail.

It was the wrong thing for Nias to say.

Mark scowled when he saw. "Plans're Patentees' business," he said. "What've women to do with anything? Planning. That's for the men to do. Women never did in England or Roanoke. What's different here?"

He had argued the other way about husbandry, only a moment before.

Nias gave him a cool look. "More than a little, Bennet. You will do well to heed the women's ideas." He motioned to Humphrey and this time they got away, leaving the carpenter gaping, his face red with anger.

Now what would happen, Humphrey wondered. Why was Mark so sure that his own ideas were the only right ones? He hadn't acted so on Roanoke. Indeed, he seemed a different person from the quiet, usually kind man they had known there. His new boldness hadn't counted for much, so far. Nias hadn't agreed to anything, had only listened.

It had taken time, though, when he should have been giving orders, arranging for the night's shelter and getting the women to think about the next meal. But then he was probably as tired of responsibility as the others were of their trail burdens.

All the loads lay where they had been happily dropped. The spinning wheel was tipped crazily on its side and Little Amby's basket, empty once more, hung from the spindle. The geese lay huddled together nearby, with heads tucked under wings, snatching untended naps.

The whole relaxed atmosphere could almost be felt, so that everyone was startled when they heard the bell. They acted at first as if they had forgot the sound of it. It hadn't been heard once in the past twelve days, because there hadn't been the need. At meal times John Brooke had had his audience at hand, for matins or evensong and brief blessings or longer ones after food.

Now it was seen that he had prepared a smooth tree stump for altar and that he had unpacked his vestments while the rest had been gossiping and planning. He crossed the grass and stood, quietly waiting. It wasn't

Lady of Roanoke

Sunday, he said to those nearest him, but they need not wait to say their prayers of thanksgiving for having been brought safely out of what might have proved great tribulation.

The colonists looked at each other, and hastily away, a little abashed for having so easily forgot their religious manners, and after the women reached out for the noisy children, a silence fell and each knelt where he stood on the lovely grass with flowers in it.

Then John Brooke said, "Let us pray."

Several hours later, when Indian hospitality had again been extended in the form of food and sleeping arrangements—the women and children in a village house and the men on mats by an enormous campfire near the felled trees—as well as shelter for the precious goods—Nias asked Humphrey to walk about with him in the twilight.

It was only a stroll to the sloping edge of the park land, where they stood listening to the sounds of evening, a little wind in the pines, the water rippling below them, the last bird calls.

Then Nias said, "There's a thing you have to know, Humphrey. Manteo didn't want to say it, so I must. It's about your manor. An you ever get it, the means will come slowly. Did you never reason, back there on Roanoke, what was behind the enmity of Towaye's people? I didn't and I'm older, so I'm sure you never realized they hated us for taking their land."

"Taking it?" Humphrey repeated, bewildered. "But

Sir Richard Grenville came first and we just . . . those were his men's huts, abandoned, that we settled in. Didn't he pay the Indians for our part of the island? Or Sir Walter?"

Nias shook his head, and Humphrey could barely see the motion in the growing dusk. "Not a sovereign." He snapped his fingers, impatiently. "Those five hundred acres each that our patron promised weren't really his to give. Not the way the Indians see it. They were here first, weren't they? And Manteo tells me that it is impossible for any chief, or family, or any section of a tribe to give up any part of Indian lands. They are held by the whole group in community ownership. So, even if Sir Richard had offered payment, they wouldn't have taken it."

Humphrey said, "Do you mean we can't stay here, Nias? Must we start back tomorrow and camp on the coast until a ship comes . . . any ship . . . that will take us back to England? Did Governor White know this when he left?"

"Nay, lad, hear me," said Nias, patiently. "Manteo wants you to have your manor. He knows what you mean because he has been in England. But while his people welcome us, the whole tribe may not be willing for us to stay on their lands. We must prove our friendship. Each Coree family is given as much ground for cultivation as their needs measure. I understand that that is the way we will be treated. They will assign us what we require to live on and to raise our food. That's all we can expect."

Lady of Roanoke

The stars were giving some light now. Nias's features were clearer. He looked anxious and worried, Humphrey thought. He had too much responsibility for one young man, all the fault of Governor White who should have remained with them and helped. He could have sent a letter just as well by the ship, telling their needs. Now they would never get those extras, the clothing and blankets and tools, no matter who brought them or when. If that should ever happen.

He, Humphrey, didn't intend to add more to Nias's worries. He had to swallow hard not to show his disappointment about having a farm right away when he said, "Eleanor told me I'd have to share what I grew and I said I would. I say it again. My new Gilling is only put a little farther off, I think. I may still hope for it? If Manteo's people make the others see that we mean no harm and that there is enough land for all of us? To sow and to reap and to make homes?"

Ananias Dare held out his hand. "Yes, Humphrey. Well spoken. And you may hope, though I'm afraid Manteo will attach some conditions. . . . But it's too early to think of those now. Before you get that far, you'll need a place to stay. No matter what arrangements are made for housing, your home is still with us, yours and Georgie's. You belong to us, as much as if you were both born Dares."

Humphrey gripped Nias's hand and held onto it a moment before he could speak. "I think Georgie had never had a proper home until he lived with us at Roanoke. Please tell Eleanor . . . give her thanks for us both. I'll help all I can. But . . ."

"Yes, speak out, boy."

"Arrangements are not my part to say but I was wondering if Eleanor may not need even more help than I can give, if the Berrys have their own place? Jane Pierce really kept the house on Roanoke even after she married Henry."

Nias laughed. "Oh, that's all settled, too. Elizabeth Glane wants to take Jane's place. She told Eleanor that if living with us got Jane a fine husband, she'd like to try her hand. As much as said that it would bring her good luck."

"It'll seem odd not to have Jane and Henry with us," said Humphrey. "I didn't know Mistress Glane very well on Roanoke."

"She asked only one thing, that we all call her Betsey, so we shan't mix up the two Elizabeths in our company."

Humphrey said, "Betsey Glane," to see how it sounded. "It suits her, doesn't it? She's quite pretty and . . ."

"And sure of her own mind," said Nias, chuckling. "Come, I think we'd better be settling to sleep. To-morrow there will be much to do."

Nias was thoughtful as he walked beside Humphrey to the campfire. The boy was so tall and had given such reliable help on the trail that it was easy to forget he was still coming out of boyhood. Mark Bennet had been too brusque today, disposing of him in those contemptuous words, as almost a bother to have in the colony. And why wouldn't his book help?

It wasn't like Mark to speak so. Something must

Lady of Roanoke

have irritated him. But he ought to realize that harmony was more than ever important.

Some day it would become clear to all that they were no longer a colony of the Queen. They were here only to save their mortal lives. But no one had voiced that yet and he'd keep his thoughts to himself until he had to speak more plainly. The colonists—nay, they were exiles—would work better without that stark truth.

MARK BENNET'S TEMPER

6

There was only one way to start work on their food supply and that was to get a corn crop in, which could be harvested by first frost in mid-October. It would provide at least one staple for winter.

Nias Dare said so, to the Patentees first, and then to the other colonists when he called the company together for general discussion the next morning.

"Manteo told me, on the trail, that his people always make two sowings of corn. You've seen their present fields, already ripe. He was sure that they would have put in a second seeding some time ago, so we will be late, but if we hasten . . ."

He was interrupted by protests against such energy, made by the less industrious.

"Haven't we been through enough, Nias? Wait until spring to plant. The Indians seem to have enough food for all."

Dion Harvie shot to his feet and glared at those who advocated delay. He was so angry he couldn't talk fast enough.

"Have you no pride? We're alive just because these people haven't killed us." He gestured toward the Indian settlement. "They could have, so we are here on their sufferance. Because they like us, though why they do, some of you . . ." He shook his head in puzzlement. "Don't you realize what that means? Of course we'll plant, before we wear out our welcome. The sooner this meeting ends, the better, so we may begin."

He was answered by a loud murmur like the hum of bees, which Nias stopped with a lifted hand. "Remember," he counseled them, "our friends see a great deal more than we realize they do. We are not within walls, so let us be cautious in our bearing. They are friendly at the moment. We'd like it to last. But we must earn it. Now, has anyone something more to add?"

It was then it became evident that those who could always be counted on for doing their share and more of any work, were divided on the subject of what should be done first. One group, for whom Mark Bennet seemed to speak, thought houses should be the first care.

"Even with logs cut," he said, " 'twill take time to

build'm. All we had to do on Roanoke was move in, with a little repair and pullin' away overgrown vines. Here we have to start with the foundation. We need to be roofed before first frost. Only one way to do that. Put up framework with saplins', cover'm with mats and live like the Indians. Don't know yet how many houses'll be needed, short of sortin' ourselves out and who's to live where . . . how to place'm. That's the first consideration, Nias Dare."

A shocked groan swept over the little company, the women looking at each other and shaking determined heads. Live like the Indians? Mark shouldn't ask it.

Humphrey was puzzled. Mark had talked for log houses last night. What had changed his mind? Was there a plot afoot to wreck the colony by dissension before they could establish anything? He looked at the faces of the Patentees in turn. Why didn't they say something to help Nias? Only Dion Harvie had spoken so far. Oh, there was Roger Prat standing up. That feckless one. How had he ever become a Patentee of Sir Walter's? When he began to talk Humphrey forgot his derision.

The man's voice was low and cultivated, and the groaning and grumbling had to stop, so he could be heard.

"We need to do both," he exhorted them, "to build and to plant. Why may we not? Some can help in one way and some another. Meantime, let the women say where they'd like the houses built and of what sort, and when they decide, that will show us where to put our place of general meeting. I . . . well, there's Johnnie, I had to bring him, he's all I've got, and I'm willing to work for two, but . . ." he turned and spoke more directly to Nias, ". . . I'll have to be shown what to do. I'm not . . . I've never done . . ."

Nias nodded his understanding and then, before he sat down, Roger added one sentence, for all. "You must realize," he said, earnestly, "that our meeting place should be close to the . . . easy to reach from every house."

They knew, startlingly, what he meant, even the most thoughtless. If the Indians ever turned against them, there should be quick access to the one place where they could all shelter together, as long as their bullets and gunpowder lasted, and then die there among friends, not alone.

Mark Bennet was standing again before Roger Prat sat down. He looked a little contemptuously at the man's fine hands, smooth and clean. They'd never known hard work. That was what Roger had meant. Mark was already exasperated and now Master Prat had said another wrong thing for his peace. It seemed easy to do.

"What've the women got to do with where we put the houses?" the carpenter asked, almost shouting. "When, in England, did we give the distaff side the say in such things? I'm the master builder here, you all know that. I don't need a lot of women to . . . to . . ."

Nias didn't let him finish. He said, firmly, "You forget, Mark, that our Queen is a woman. She has a great deal to say at times. I think you do need the mind of the distaff side, here, the whole seventeen. It is they who will be keeping the houses and if they are comfortable and satisfied—er, I mean if the doors and windows are exactly where they think they should be, all of us will be happy." He smiled at Eleanor and she nodded, energetically. "You'd be outvoted, man, an I asked for a count. A bachelor should keep on good terms with the women."

Doors and windows meant log houses and the whole company laughed, and Mark's scowl went deeper.

Thomas Warner, not a Patentee, spoke unexpectedly. He was a tall, thin Oxford scholar, a mathematician of some repute, but neither he nor his wife Joan put on any airs, so he was listened to with respect. He drew some bits of paper from his doublet and held them in one hand while he stroked his fine-pointed brown beard with the other.

"House plans," he said, holding up the papers. "A few measurements at least, that I figured by the campfire when I couldn't sleep last night. If you'd appoint Bennet and me as a building committee, Nias, we could wait upon the ladies and get their ideas. It would be a fair start, I think."

Nias beamed at him. "It's done," he said.

He looked round at the whole company then, as they sat facing him on the flower-starred grass, in groups right, left and center. "I don't like to give orders," he said, gravely, "but you can't all work at each thing we take in hand, at the same time, at least not until the houses are begun. I could make a few assignments and see how haply all goes in the next few days. Work should go well if each person knows his portion and does it."

Even the grumpiest ones had to admit that that was as fair a way to begin as any, to better their situation. So they sat back to listen with more grace, but there was uproar again, the minute Nias spoke a name.

"To take charge of the planting, Humphrey Hall, with such others as . . ."

"Nias, Nias Dare," Mark Bennet shouted, shaking a fist. "An you make playacting of this thing, we'll all starve. That's all it is, putting this . . . this boy in charge of our fields."

What *can* be the matter with him, Humphrey wondered, and not knowing where to look. He's angry about having to deal with the women, of course, but I don't come into that.

Thomas Warner, suave and controlled, came to the rescue again. "We have no fields of our own, Master Bennet. Will not have. Only the use of enough land to raise what we need. That is tribal law. I have inquired."

His emphasis on *Master* made Mark flush.

Nor did Nias help the carpenter's humiliation when he said, firmly, "Humphrey can indeed take a man's part here, I must remind all of you. And I'd wager he is the best planter among us. Manteo's mother taught him the Indian way on Roanoke. And he was a good pupil because he wanted to learn, so I doubt not that we shall all benefit. The children could help him as they are able. They like to be where he is, so they will be looked after at the same time. Where, then, is your quarrel, Mark? You'll have your hands full. We—the other Patentees and I—will see to the rest."

It was a clear invitation to Mark Bennet to attend to his own business or to leave the meeting if he couldn't keep still, which he ignored. He sat down, muttering.

They would need diggers, loggers and water carriers, Nias went on, searchers in the woods to bring in wild fruit in order not to let the Indians bear all the immediate food responsibility. Six men were named to help prepare the fields for sowing when the Indians had been consulted. Four others, who said they'd like to, were detailed to learn how to make the pottery dishes and bowls which the Corees used commonly, if the Indian women were willing to disclose the secret of their skill.

When the meeting ended, Roger Prat promptly borrowed Little Amby's basket and another one and took his John and the other small boys to look for fruit.

Humphrey, with Georgie Howe and Lion at his heels, spoke to Nias before going to the Indian settlement to see Manteo and Mary. Georgie had strict orders to collar Lion if any of the village dogs showed fight, and Humphrey attempted to make sure that the little boy understood the harm of quarreling in general. He wasn't certain how much Georgie had observed at the meeting.

"It wastes time, for one thing, when people fight," said Humphrey earnestly, "especially when there is a lot of work to do. And it is bad for their dispositions."

"I don't know that word," said Georgie.

"It's the way you feel, the way your habit is, whether you talk crossly or pleasantly to others and don't let your temper get best place every time you disagree with another's idea."

"Then I'm not the one you should be talking to," said the little boy, cheerfully. "That old Mark Bennet needs it more. He was nice on Roanoke, some. He made the lean-to for your heifer and he helped Henry at the fort and not a cross word, ever. Now, look at him this morning. Why's he put out with you?"

"I've been wondering about that myself, a little," said Humphrey. "Something has happened to him."

Lion at that moment bounded ahead, barking at a chattering squirrel clinging to a tree, just out of his reach. Humphrey spoke sternly and Lion came to heel again. He said, "Did you know, Georgie, that Mistress Glane is going to live with us at the Dares, when their house is ready?"

"No," said Georgie, "nobody told me. She's nice. I'm glad we're going to be there, too. Just like on Roanoke, except that I wish my goose hadn't died."

"Maybe Mistress Harvie will give you another one, when she has her next hatching. It could be, though, that Nias won't let us have as many animals as we had there. He'll not mind Lion, of course, because he's a good watchdog."

MARK BENNET'S TEMPER

"But I want a pet, too," Georgie argued.

"I'll speak to Nias," Humphrey promised, and felt very grown-up. Georgie treated him as a father, had indeed substituted him for the older George, dead these three years.

Georgie said, a little pensively, "It won't be exactly like Roanoke, though, whatever animals we have, because William is the baby in the cradle now. He's a cross one. I like Virginia better. I'm going to marry her, when we get big."

"So?" said Humphrey. "Have you asked her, yet? That's the custom, I believe, so she'll wait for you, or some other man might get there first."

"Who's to do that?" Georgie asked, scornfully. "She's only a baby, yet. I've got to wait. But she better like it, when I do ask her."

"Lots of time to change your mind," said Humphrey. "Suppose the Viccars baby that's coming should be a girl?"

"Why should I think of maybe changing my mind, Humphrey? I already know. Besides, Little Amby could get a baby brother."

He leaped ahead again, involuntarily, because Lion gave a great lunge and was off, leading them into the village, where there was a tumult of barking, welcoming voices and leaping dogs, but no fights, only waving tails and noses-to-noses in the dust cloud they had kicked up. Lion was blood of their blood and welcome.

It was a better village than the one on Roanoke which Humphrey had visited so many times. But the greetings and the friendliness were the same. The women crowded round Humphrey in welcome. When he found that a little black puppy at his feet was in danger of being stepped on, he stooped, almost automatically, and gathered it up. The little thing settled contentedly into the crook of his left arm and the women laughed and pointed at it.

Then Manteo appeared and the women brought out food and left them to begin their parley about the land and the planting.

Mary was delighted that her pupil had been so honored by the colonists and said so, in her halting English. To Manteo she spoke rapidly in their own tongue, which Humphrey, try as he might, could not yet follow swiftly, though he knew she was asking and urging something.

Manteo interpreted, somewhat hesitantly. "My mother is having an anxiety for your understanding about the land. Did the Patentee Dare explain that it is not mine or hers to give or sell? But some day . . ." The young Indian's eyes gleamed with promise of the future.

Here was confirmation of what Eleanor had repeated, Humphrey thought, without explaining how it could come about. It was strange Manteo could be so sure, could offer him hope. It did not occur to Humphrey, until long time afterward, what other way there could be, when the land could not be gifted or sold, for him to acquire a farm.

Manteo dismissed the future for the present,

abruptly. "Come and I will show you the fields that our chief says you may work. You have seen . . ." he asked, as they walked, Humphrey still cuddling the black puppy, "how we plant the beans so that they climb the corn as it grows and we save the work of cutting poles for them?"

"I have seen," said Humphrey. "And that the pumpkins and the squashes, too, are set around the edges of the fields."

"There is seed enough for all," said Manteo, "if you like to eat those. Our chief has ordered it to be given."

With Mary behind the order, Humphrey was sure. He felt laughter surging up from his stomach in a great gasp, which would affront Manteo if he did not stop it. So he stooped to find a pebble in his moccasin, to hide the spasm. How *young* he had been, not to think of their need of seed, more than the few small ears of corn that he had saved from his last garden at Roanoke. Just let Mark Bennet find that out. These fields ready to harvest that they had passed were larger than he had dreamed. Manteo would not understand his amusement at his own stupidity, so he struggled that the Indian might not see.

Manteo waited patiently, watching. More shoes must be made for the young Englishman, he thought, because he never took care of his own needs, but only those of others—so many others, from the little Lady of Roanoke, and every child, to this puppy. If it had been hurt, there were plenty more in the litter. Those moccasins had been worn too much.

Lady of Roanoke

"You like that little dog?" Manteo asked, when they went on again.

"I hadn't thought of it," Humphrey confessed. "It seemed in danger underfoot, so I picked it up, that's all. I have Lion, Manteo, your mother's gift to me. He is the best watchdog I ever knew."

"But Georgie has only your dog to play with," Manteo hinted.

"The child should have something of his own to pet, to look after," Humphrey agreed, "especially because his goose died. I think he fed it too well. We talked about a pet for him on the way here, but we'll be living with the Dares again and Nias should help decide . . . I don't know about our having two dogs," he ended, lamely.

"From our sheep, a little lamb, then," Manteo urged, "and the dog, too, I think. You will need more than one watcher in your houses."

"What do you mean, Manteo? Surely there can be no danger hereabout? For any of us?"

Manteo looked mournful. "I did not mean to make you fear, it is only that we . . . we protect ourselves. There are other tribes, not friendly to us. Unless they have spies they know nothing about you, yet. But some day they might. The Tuscaroras are most to be feared. A dog in every colonist's house would not be too many, but the English ladies would not like that, I think."

Humphrey grinned. "No, they wouldn't. But there are the Harvie geese. They make enough noise for several dogs, when they are disturbed."

A slow, unwonted smile moved Manteo's mouth a little. "Yes," he said, "there are those geese."

They talked during the rest of Humphrey's observation trip, about the tools he would need, what he would sow, when he would reap, harvest by harvest for the colonists. Apparently the great acreage of cleared forest land had lain fallow, for it was covered with weed growth, that had been cut and left to dry.

Manteo took all of it in, in one sweeping gesture. "This, to be burned away."

The ground would need a lot of breaking up, Humphrey was sure, but he did not say so.

Georgie was speechless when he was told he could carry the little black puppy back to camp.

But there were Little Amby and Johnnie Prat and the other children to think about, if they should feel Georgie was favored. Nias's position as Chief Patentee might explain the gift of a dog to Georgie because he lived in his house. But even while he was thinking of the argument, Humphrey knew it wouldn't count at all with any colony child.

All the way back to the camp, slowed by Lion, who hadn't wanted to leave his friends in the Indian village, Humphrey pondered his report to Nias and the problem of pets for the colony children. What else could be substituted for dogs besides lambs that would lose their attraction when they grew up into sheep, and no longer be pets?

TOM-THE-LUTE SINGS AND OBSERVES

7

Humphrey was disappointed when he and Georgie came through the thin screen of trees that separated the colony's site from the fields and the Indian village, to see that he wouldn't be able to talk to Nias at once, as he had hoped.

The people had separated to do their appointed work and one matter was going on that he hadn't heard planned, earlier.

Stones had been collected in a sheltered spot close to the trees at the near end of the open space, and Richard Berry, brother of Henry, and several helpers were building an outdoor cooking place, fitting the pieces together with some thick mud, as fast as they could be dressed for snug placement. The big iron stew-pot stood by, ready to be filled and perched above the new hearth. Evidently the women were determined on cooking as soon as possible, whether or not they had roofs.

John Sampson and Billy Wythers had been dispatched to pile up wood and brush for the nightly campfire. That was to be their job until it was no longer needed.

Farther off, almost midway of the park land that looked toward the blue hills, Tom-the-Lute Jones sat on a tree stump and strummed. His baby daughter Megan slept in a basket bed at his feet, and Miss Virginia Dare stood on the next stump, the one John Brooke had used for an altar, doing pirouettes in time to the music, for a circle of admiring small boys who had returned from berrying. Their heaped baskets, protected by a square of cloth, sat beside the Jones baby's bed.

Tom's wife, who had been Margaret Lawrence, was with the other women.

They stood in a tight-formed circle around Nias, Henry Berry and Thomas Warner, paying no attention to Mark Bennet, who hovered outside the little corporation. He was still scowling but listened intently to the shrill, often staccato bits of talk. How anyone could make out a thing from that chorus, Humphrey couldn't imagine. But the women were enjoying it, that was clear even from his distance.

Lady of Roanoke

Power had slipped out of Mark's hands by that
unfortunate remark of his—*I don't need the women*—
and now they were showing him that it was he who
wasn't needed. Humphrey chuckled and wondered how
long their snubbing would last. It was plain though that
he himself would have to wait his turn with Nias. How
long, say? If the women did any real deciding by mid-
day there'd be a foundation to set in the afternoon.
Wouldn't they start building the meeting house first?
Nias would have to be present for that, make a ceremony of it, maybe.

So, how would he, Humphrey, keep busy while
he waited for Nias to be free? He could gather the
children together and keep them out of mischief. He
could, an he wanted to.

Meantime, Tom-the-Lute was always good company, and he seemed the only person in sight at ease
with all his world, and enjoying it. Humphrey made his
way slowly in Tom's direction, with Georgie still following, in and out between the cast-off doublets belonging to the men who labored at trimming logs and
at the hearth, with the ruffled cuffs of their shirtsleeves
pushed elbow high. The stone pile was growing. They
didn't need more help there.

Tom's tune was a gay, lilting thing, enough to
make anyone want to dance.

> *Can you make me a cambric shirt*
> *Without a seam, or fine needlework?*
> *Then a teasalum, tasalum, templum.*

Can you wash it in a well
Where water ne'er ran nor never fell?
  Can you?
Then a teasalum, tasalum, templum.

Can you dry it on a thorn
That never was, since Adam's morn?
  Oh, can you?
Then a teasalum, tasalum, templum.

There were a dozen verses with equally impossible situations set forth in every one. And the giddy refrain was apt to go around and around in one's head all day if it wasn't resisted.

Virginia was enjoying it and her audience, the little mischief. Humphrey watched her with anxious thought. She wouldn't have been the only girl child of her age in the colony, had the Harvie's babe, born ten days after Virginia, lived. Now Margery Harvie was left with only her geese to tend—she did well with them—but Eleanor Dare had William to look after. What would happen to Virginia, already too fond of her own way? Mayhap Betsey Glane would know what to do.

Tom looked up as the two boys approached and made to put the lute down, ready to talk, but Humphrey shook his head and sat down on half the stump when Tom moved over and went on strumming.

Can you buy me an acre of land
Between the salt water and the wide sea strand?

Can you? Then please do.
And a tiralum, flummalum, lummy.

"And that's enough," Tom said. He laid the lute by and yawned and asked, "Doesn't it strike you, Humphrey-lad, that what we're trying to do here is about as impossible as my song's verses? Whoever made a cambric shirt, or one of fair silk, without sewing it? Figured out, have you, how we're going to raise enough food for seventy-odd folks here? *And* build'm houses? Need twelve for the married folks alone. Those malcontents who stayed on the coast did us a kindness, going off. I hadn't thought on't until now. We haven't to feed'm."

Humphrey said, countering the pessimism, "We've been given the use of all the land we can work. If we may just get a crop in now, and have a good rain, I'll show you cambric shirts. You'll have to sing something else."

Tom could say only "Promising miracles, eh?" before Virginia spied Georgie. She jumped down from her stump and came running toward him. "You brought me a little dog," she shouted. "Give it to me, Georgie. I want to hold it. Right now." She held out her hands, ready to receive the black puppy as her right.

Too many things had been done for her because she was the colony's only little girl, Humphrey thought, and sighed for his own past errors of that kind.

Georgie backed away from her, tripped on a small stone hidden in the grass and fell, and Humphrey swooped and caught the little dog before it was hurt. He might better have left it to its fate underfoot in the Indian village, he thought, ruefully.

"She can't have it," Georgie screamed, from the ground, as soon as he could get his breath. "Don't you give it to her, Humphrey. That puppy's mine. You mayn't touch it, Virginia. Manteo gave it to me."

Tom yawned again and took up his lute, after a glance at his baby, who slept placidly on. The quarreling hadn't wakened her. He grinned at Humphrey over the heads of the noisy children.

"Women!" he remarked. "Young Virginia is only like the rest, as mine will be when she finds her feet. Look at their mothers, down there bedeviling Bennet. Let a man once open his mouth—what will our houses be like? Seventeen different ideas, but no mats on sapling frames, an I was wagerin'. Nothin' to bet with, here. What's a shilling any more? Somethin' to show our grandchildren as a curiosity."

"What need of shillings when there's naught to buy?" Humphrey asked, crisply.

He held Virginia in his arms now, soothing her, and at the same time instructing Georgie. "Take the little dog back to Manteo. I'll not have quarreling over it. You are to say that until we have a house—the Dares' house—we'd like him to keep the puppy for us, safely. He will not think you are giving it back for good and all. I could have refused it at once, an I had chosen. You may take Lion with you, but don't stay over there. Lion will want to."

Lady of Roanoke

Georgie walked away slowly, shoulders drooping, but holding the puppy carefully. Lion followed him, tail low.

Tom said, "You sound as if you'd fathered'm both, and you only seventeen."

Humphrey grinned. "I'm growing up, some. And I've helped raise the two of them," he reminded Tom, "living with Nias and Eleanor the way I have. It's going to be the same here, though we'll have Mistress Glane to help."

"For how long?" Tom asked, his eyes twinkling. "She is most comely. I think rector sir would agree."

Humphrey ignored that invitation to gossip. He set Virginia down, smoothed the curls round her face and pulled her muslin cap straight. "Go and play now," he urged, "see, Little Amby is waiting for you. The puppy will come back one of these days, but it really is Georgie's. That's truth. I was there when Manteo gave it to him. Never mind, you will have a pet of your own an you wait for it, little Lady of Roanoke. Heed now, what your Humphrey says." He gave her a gentle push.

The child's lovely eyes widened and she gave the big boy an odd look before she scampered off.

Tom shook his head, watching the little boys welcoming Virginia back. "That's one female knows what she wants and means to have it," he remarked.

Humphrey spread his hands, without speech, and sat down again by Tom, looking out toward those far blue hills. In the short time they had been in this place

—it could still be counted by hours, so short a span it was—he had taken peace from that lovely view, out over the valley with its gurgling stream. He was satisfied even more, each time he looked that way, that he would have known this to be the good place waiting, somewhere, even if it hadn't been so close to Manteo's people.

Tom strummed the lute again but didn't start another song, and to that muted obbligato they talked.

Humphrey said, "I'll be glad when the seventeen decide what we may have and we can raise the houses—start living in them. But Indian ones will take longer than logs. When could enough mats be woven to cover so many frames? And who's to do it? Our women don't know the way of weaving mats yet. The Indians dye some of the dried rushes they use and make patterns, same as for baskets. A slow manner of work. And Tom, look you, Manteo's people themselves expected us to want logs or they'd not have cut so many, ready for a start. Mark Bennet made it clear in the meeting that he was for saplings and mats. Yet he talked most differently last night, when there was only Nias and me to hear. I can't think why he'd change overnight and be so set in the opposite way."

"No?" Tom answered, with a lazy smile. "Think on't, lad. Did you never see Nias work a matter by contraries? With Eleanor? You are overyoung with all your height, an you haven't marked that. Women have to be managed. Ain't in their nature to be direct. So . . .?"

Lady of Roanoke

He grinned with Humphrey at the boy's dawning comprehension.

"You mean Mark was afraid they'd want saplings and mats, so he talked in favor? To turn them against?"

Tom nodded. "Nias almost spoiled his scheme when he said right out to let'm say where doors and windows should go. You don't have to decide on openings for a mat house. Shift one, and light comes in, wherever you want it. All outdoors, too, of course. Haven't you thought on't, boy, at all? 'Twas plain to me."

"No," said Humphrey, "no, Tom, I didn't, only to wonder why Mark Bennet is so crossgrained. He could argue for mat houses without growling at the women the way he did."

"Got to take his temper out on something." He stopped strumming, and frowned. "Funny, how a little power grips a man. Mark wants something more in that line, I think. Not high as a Patentee . . . anyone knows that'd be impossible, because they signed up in England as property owners or with other responsible standing, and put some money in, too. Maybe it's just a little extra attention, or to be boss of something. Don't know what it'd be, here . . . just the way it strikes me. Some people can't bear for their good work to be taken for granted. And it's becoming clear to some here that things don't have to come by bein' born to'm, maybe, all being more equal in the New World."

Humphrey began to grin and Tom wanted to know why.

"I said as much, that last part anyway, to John and

Billy before we left Roanoke. They hadn't thought of it . . . being *young*, maybe."

Tom wanted to laugh at that word *young*, but he looked at Humphrey as an equal in years and spoke so. "'Twouldn't occur to some folks, ever, their habit of being how they're born, so strong. While I'm thinkin' this may be Mark's trouble, 'twouldn't worry me for a minute. I've married me the wife I wanted and what's there more to ask for? 'Ceptin' a family as lovely as their mother. Got the start of that, already."

He stooped to smooth out a wrinkle in little Megan's blanket. It had been ingeniously fashioned by her mother from an old, worn wool shirt of Tom's . . . the best parts of it would last a lot longer, she said.

Tom picked up the lute again and started strumming. "A wife to love and a song to sing," he murmured softly to his strings.

"So you've got my testimony, lad," he went on, to Humphrey, "life looks good to me from right here on this stump."

Humphrey said, "It's reasonable. But people aren't, always. Mark, now. Yours is a new idea about him. I should think *he'd* think he's got all the power he needs, right now. I've been looking at fields this morning and calculating crops the way my book says, while you have watched your child and strummed, with a mind to bend on what's underneath the things people say. So, Mr. John Thomas Jones, tell me, an you can, where Roger Prat got *his* gumption? He's hid it well, so far."

"Surprised a few folks this morning, he did," said

Lady of Roanoke

Tom, grinning his appreciation of that. "More'n a few, likely. He's an odd body, but likeable when you know him. We talked a little on the ship, but afterward he kept to himself, he and the boy, and I was busy, some, m'self, about then."

Humphrey chuckled. Tom's desertion of his place in the crew of *The Lion*, to cast his lot with the colonists on account of Margaret Lawrence's fair comeliness, had provided much colony gossip after John White sailed. Tom had stayed with the Dares until the banns could be read, for the wedding.

"Nias should put Prat to teaching," Tom went on. "He knows plants and trees and animals. Might be useful for the children to learn what's poisonous and what ain't, round in the woods. Tell'm, an you get the chance, Humphrey."

That good occasion didn't come until evening.

Decisions took far longer than they needed to, that day, some thought, just because the women were enjoying their new right to have a part in them. It seemed log houses were the only practical thing and they followed Mark around the green when he began to step off the space, using Thomas Warner's figures. They had to be shown how much room there'd be for each little dwelling and how it would be placed.

He had stopped scowling but his genial Roanoke manner was not restored, and Humphrey, noting that, felt the more sure that Tom-the-Lute had given him the key to the man's demeanor. Maybe, when the building really began, he'd feel himself the big man in the colony, after all.

TOM-THE-LUTE SINGS AND OBSERVES

Altogether that day was a wearing experience for the whole colony, as bad as one on the trail, but when the housing plan was settled they were contented that it had had to be so.

By late afternoon, everyone having even some small imagination, the power to see with the mind's eyes, knew how the green—that favorite open space of Humphrey's—might appear when it had houses around it, connecting paths and flowers—"as near to a garden at home as may be," said Joan Warner. "My Tom said he'd see to't."

Besides the twelve houses for the families and the Long House, using the Indians' term for their meeting place, they'd need a storeroom for the staples they meant to raise and a shelter at least, for Henry Berry's anvil. Two larger log huts were planned for the bachelors and the widowers with sons, with two of the childless couples, one in each, to manage the housekeeping for them.

There were still arguments, here and there, about everything. It would tax their energies before that much building could be done, even in a reasonable time. How many of the men knew how to raise a log house?

No mention was made of spinsters. In accommodating fashion each had already found work for herself with the families.

Humphrey listened to the chattering groups and wondered why the three single women hadn't yet found husbands as Jane Pierce and Margaret Lawrence had done, on Roanoke. Finicking, belike, because the eligible men so outnumbered them.

Lady of Roanoke

By evening everything seemed to have been talked over thoroughly when Nias assembled them after their meal, to accept or reject the day's decisions—made by the women but read out by Mark Bennet. They had graciously yielded him that. This time there was a vote —a real count of all the men and women taken by the affirmative standing up. It was made in deep silence.

When Nias said, in a relieved voice, "There is no dissent," John Brooke raised his hands and gave the company and their plan a fervent blessing, together.

Humphrey had a feeling of awe and guilty gratitude, as he stood waiting, afterward, to speak to Nias. He was the only one of that whole company who was likely to achieve the thing he had come for. If Manteo's mysterious plan came true.

The others were not settling where they had thought to, when leaving England. They hadn't found any gold—would not, probably, here in this place of fields and forests and water. They were here because they couldn't go back to England and it was safer to be inland. Their every act from now on would be self-preservation, merely, without any other aim in life. Unless one of course, Mark Bennet, persisted in waiting to get power. Who was there to impress, here? Only the other colonists, and himself.

But the country was beautiful and the woods were full of wild food. The children would have some means of learning and all could have a good life together, an they willed it to be. Humphrey was already sure of that willing, for himself.

SEEDS FOR THE FUTURE

8

After Nias had seen Eleanor and Betsey and the children safely started on the path to the Indian village to settle for sleep, he came to the campfire where Humphrey waited and they walked again, out to the edge of the green where it sloped gently down to the water.

Behind them was the pleasant, gossipy buzz of voices as the other men lingered in the sweet-smelling twilight. The women had cooked a meal at the new hearth, and the wood smoke and rich gravy scents mingled with the natural smell of crushed grass and the new-cut pine and cedar logs.

Below was the soft ripple of the stream.

Lady of Roanoke

Humphrey said, "Happen there's watercress in a pool there. Tomorrow I'll find a way down and see, if there's a deer path I can follow, or any other. Something fresh tasting would liven up the stew."

Nias laughed. "That you can still think of food after a meal proves me right in assigning you the planting." Then he asked, more briskly, "How did your talk go, this morning, with Manteo? I hope you made my manners for me, explaining why I haven't yet been to see the chief? I doubt that Eleanor has thought of it."

"How could she, Nias? I didn't think of it, either. I said never a word about you. No excuses. Nothing. I'll tell you how it was."

Nias was carrying his long cape—all the men had them, as was the fashion when they left England—ready for wrapping up in it by the campfire when he should be ready for sleep.

He spread it now and said, "Let's sit. You sound as if you had more than a little to say. But manners are important, Humphrey, anywhere, as I shouldn't have to remind you. You were taught well at Gilling."

Humphrey drew his knees up, clasped his hands around them and leaned forward before he answered the rebuke.

"Nothing happened this morning in the Indians' usual way, Nias," he said. "It was more like . . . an I was at home in Yorkshire and had gone a-calling at your house, or on the Langleys at Beverly, just neighbors. All the Indians we knew at Roanoke and more beside came swarming out and the dogs welcomed Lion. It was a great doing, altogether."

SEEDS FOR THE FUTURE

"That I can't doubt," said Nias, a little stiffly. "A show of friendliness by the Indians is good and valuable right now. But, no ceremony? That's strange. I hope they were not offended that I . . . or one other Patentee, Dion Harvie for choice, was not with you. I had no thought of it when I let you go."

He put his head in his hands, bent over and groaned. "I *should* have gone, myself, but how could I? How *could* I? The absence of formality, when this is the home of a chief, worries me, Humphrey. Am I to suppose then, that nothing was accomplished, only frolicking? That we have lost another day in starting on our plans for raising food? It was your youth, no doubt, that made them hesitate to treat with you."

Humphrey was astonished. Nias's voice was discouraged. What had come over the man? His hands rested on his knees now, his face, dimly seen, a blank. Granted he was tired. Granted he had a lot of responsibility. But he was not old, only thirty-five.

And then came the swift-stabbing thought, the answer. Nias must be realizing as well as had he, in spite of his youth, that no matter what the colonists did, they had no future here, no aim but self-preservation, that they must think only of the necessity to keep alive. Why did he doubt the Indians' continued help, feel they must exert themselves far more than they had on Roanoke to keep their goodwill? What could he say to stir Nias? Something strong was needed, but there was nothing he could think of better than the truth, the morning's happening.

"No, Nias, 'tis not as you think at all, else why are

we to have all the Indians' fallow ground to put in our own crop?"

Nias stirred. His hands moved to hug his knees as Humphrey's did. He shook his head to and fro, as if something obscured his vision, before he said, unbelievingly, "All? We are?"

"Yes, Nias, 'tis so. It has been hard for me to wait this full day to tell you, while you settled all the *ayes* and *nays*, that were offered you on so many matters."

"There were a good many, Humphrey, too many, I think." He bowed his head again on his knees and was silent long enough to seem asleep. When he did rouse, he said, "Now, to the planting. What . . . you *did* go to see Manteo this morning?"

Humphrey felt as if he had just received a good douse of cold water. What was wrong with Nias? He spoke as if he had not listened at all to what had already been said on the matter, did not recall his impatience with what he thought a lost day with the planting. Too tired, no doubt. Best ignored, Humphrey thought.

So he said, "I'm still overyoung, Nias, to be head of the planting. Mark was right. I forgot about seeds, except those ears I brought from Roanoke. We are to have beans, to climb up the cornstalks, and pumpkins and squash to put in round the edges. Mark will have to make us a form to dry the slices on when they ripen, the way Mary does. And . . ."

Nias interrupted Humphrey's eager race toward harvest, seeming to have recovered his memory, some-

SEEDS FOR THE FUTURE

what. "Didn't they ask you for anything? In return for use of the ground and the gift of seed? Manteo said nothing about his plan for you . . . for your farm?"

Humphrey chuckled. "Naught but that I could hope for it. And I doubt not but that Mary told the chief we were to be given the seeds. When have they ever asked us for return, no matter what it is they have done for us? It is not their way, surely you recall that, Nias."

"And you were not presented to the old chief?"

"No, I didn't see him."

Nias shook his head. "Strange. I don't understand it. I thought . . . well, never mind. You and Manteo must have said a great deal this morning, one to the other. Go on, Humphrey. You are not yet come to the end, are you? Speak, boy." He drew a long, painful sigh.

"There is one thing we did not talk of, but I have thought of it alone. Mark Bennet should ask Manteo how to place our houses . . . he can say better than anyone, whether the dwellings should be made to face the forest or be built back to back. No matter what any colonist's opinion is, that should be seen to."

"It is a good idea," said Nias. "I will speak to Mark. And . . . there is more?"

"I have told you all that was arranged about the fields, but Georgie needs a thing decided. About a pet, a dog, especially."

"A dog?" Nias asked, apprehensively.

He seemed more awake now, and Humphrey rushed on with the little boy's need, remembering Nias's

Lady of Roanoke

growing restiveness on Roanoke at the sight and sound of a large goose, Lion and the heifer.

"Only a puppy. Georgie does need a pet to take the place of his goose."

Nias groaned. "Poor Eleanor and Betsey," he said. "It will have to be provided for . . . a place to sleep. I doubt it will be let in the house . . . when we get one."

Humphrey took heart from his tone and told the rest of the story. Nias managed a chuckle at the neat way he had solved the children's quarrel and at the same time had got rid of the little black dog. "I hated to send her back," he finished, "but it just wouldn't do . . . not now."

Nias rose and began pacing, restlessly, leaving the cape, and Humphrey joined him.

"My head hurts," he complained, "and I seem over-drowsy for the time of evening. But I must let you have your talk out, Humphrey, when you've waited so long, as you say. Every member of the colony has a right to be heard, even the women. Colony! What a word! We severed all our rights and obligations, I verily believe, by leaving Roanoke as we did, though it was wise for safety's sake. I do not expect John White to return, and he was our last link with England. We are fugitives, really, Humphrey. Have you realized that? We can never expect to carry out the terms of our Patent from Sir Walter . . . these people are no more bound to respect what nine men decide for them hereafter . . . than . . . than . . . But as long as they believe our decisions are binding for them, for just a little while longer, until we are at least housed, for the sake of the women and children, I'll let them think so. There, I didn't mean to burden you with my worry. What was it I meant to ask you?"

He put a hand to his head, over his eyes, pressed and then resumed the pacing, Humphrey keeping step.

"Ah yes, does Georgie know about the lamb Manteo offered?"

"No, Nias, he doesn't. He stayed to play with the Indian children and the lamb was offered me when Manteo and I went to look at the fields. They lie partly between here and the village and beyond it, at the back. Eastward. The weeds were cut some time ago and they are now dried and ready to burn off. The ground looks most particularly hard to me, Nias, and shan't the burning add to the hardness? I'd like some rain if we were already roofed. Are you going to be able to spare only six men to help with the fields, Nias, think you?"

When he spoke, Nias seemed again not to have been listening. He said, "Of course lambs grow up to be sheep, but the women were talking today, among their many matters, of spinning and weaving wool—new clothes for everybody. They saw a hand loom, belonging to Mary, in the village last night. They understand how to weave, some do, from doing it in England, but none has ever used such a primitive one as hers seems." He chuckled, faintly. "They want Mark Bennet to copy it. I suppose he will, when he finds the time, because he got his way about the houses."

Humphrey said, "Nias, an I could wager anything,

Lady of Roanoke

I'd win that you didn't hear what I asked you, about more help in the fields. I take it, though, that Miss Virginia will be given the lamb when it comes? She will own it?"

"You may take it that way, Humphrey, but no word to her about it, beforehand, mind. About help for you, after I have been properly presented to the chief tomorrow, I will suggest that some of their women be sent to show you what to do, to avoid clumsiness and thus delay the work. It is the custom that they cultivate the fields, so I wonder if our men will feel demeaned by taking the direction of women? They have no choice, in our circumstances, so I hope they will see that. Strange, about the Indians' generosity with the land and the gift of seeds, too. I had pictured bargaining with the chief."

"They asked nothing," Humphrey insisted. "I told you. But we could offer something."

"What have we to give?"

There it was again, that hopeless, discouraged tone in Nias's voice. It made Humphrey conscious of his own weariness. How could he battle the man's state of mind?

They paced silently a moment or two longer, then Nias said, "We ought to find our places and sleep. There is no telling what the morrow will bring. We should be ready to meet it. I'll speak to Mark before I lie down, about seeking Manteo's advice as to placing the houses. Come!"

They had almost reached the campfire where some

of the men were already lying on their mats, composed and quiet, when Humphrey remembered the other matter, enjoined upon him by Tom. He thought to let it go, wait a more convenient time, but felt a strange urgency, too, so he plucked at Nias's sleeve, drew him back a little way and whispered.

"One more idea, that I almost forgot. Tom Jones knows Roger Prat. He said he should be put to teaching. He is most learned in plants and . . ."

Nias said, a little impatiently, "Yes, boy, I know. And Warner for sums, the rector for Latin and Tom himself for singing. All we need is pupils and we'd have a college. I had thought to make Roger master of all our guns, too. To keep them in order for use any minute. And to tally all our stores in common. He knows much more than is appreciated. He will be useful."

Humphrey said, "So it was done before my asking. I am glad Roger will have a good part in the colony, when I had thought him feckless. He seems a gentleman."

"A sad one," Nias confirmed. "He lost his wife the same year that a relative schemed away most of his lands, and his house in London. None of his property was entailed, so he sold what he had left and joined us. Not much for the better. He is grateful for your care of young Johnnie."

"It was nothing," said Humphrey. "Mayhap he will marry again, an one of these unbespoke would have him."

"They could do worse," Nias said. Then he

changed the topic in hand so abruptly that Humphrey felt as though his thoughts might be wandering again. "I cannot deny that our little Lady of Roanoke needs some little girls to play with." He snapped his fingers. "That's what we can offer, Humphrey. If I had gone to see about the fields, it might have come out. Better for us to suggest than for the Indians to be obliged to ask. Why not invite their children to attend our college? Learning to speak our tongue and learning about our ways hasn't hurt Manteo. Well, we shall see. Good night to you, Humphrey-lad. What a day! I should call it a blessed day that began so uncommon ugly."

A PLANT FOR HEALING

9

Humphrey had more than food in mind when he stirred early the next morning to seek for a path down to the stream in the valley. He would feel himself back in England again to find watercress there. He pictured the clear stream at home where he had gathered a handful many a time.

There was good swimming at Gilling, too. The nights were cool on this high ground, but walking on the trail and working in the sun had made his body yearn for soap and water.

How now! He snapped his fingers in annoyance, as he prowled along the slope below the green where he and Nias had talked last night. He hadn't thought to bring a clean shirt with him. Eleanor knew where they were, in one of the chests carried so laboriously inland. No matter. He was on his way. Better to go on. As soon as the men stirred there would be the day's duties pressing.

He zigzagged downward until he came to a narrow but clearly defined path. It could be a deer run or worn by the Indians, mayhap used by both. It wound between the trees, easy to walk on, clear of stones and weeds, but there were no signs in the packed earth to tell who ran that way or stepped warily along. Here and there a tree root had been uncovered where the path crossed it and the ground was worn away beyond, making steps.

The clean state of the path made the disappointment with the stream the sharper when Humphrey reached it. The uninviting dull brown color was bad enough, but it was choked with rushes, too, which grew thickly along the banks and invaded the water. There might be a good stony bottom but it would take time and much tedious labor to clean out that rankly growing vegetation and free the banks enough to allow stepping in and out of any natural pool he might uncover. And over all was a heavy odor of decay.

He beat along the bank for half an hour, ranging some distance in both directions from the spot where the path led down, and found the rocky fall which accounted for the pleasant sound heard above. But its cleaner water was too shallow even for the children to swim there, so he returned to his starting point.

A PLANT FOR HEALING

There, only because he was looking for it, he found watercress, almost choked out by the coarser plants. He plucked some, binding it in a ragged bunch with a long grass stem before he laid it carefully by on a tree root.

With the hunting knife he always carried he cut a slender sapling and trimmed it for a measuring stick. It would tell him two things, the depth at the place where he meant to improve Nature's gift, and the kind of bottom. There was mud on the butt when he took the pole from the water, but there must be stone or rock below it. He had felt a hardness. And the stream was only comfortably deep, barely over his knees, when he measured the mark of it against his height. The fall of the land down the valley explained the rank spread and sluggish flow here.

There would be no better time than now, early and alone, to begin the job he had rapidly planned while tramping the water course. He took off his clothes, piling them carefully under the tree where he had left the cress, weighted with a loose stone.

He stepped in a little gingerly, not surprised to find it so cold. That was because of the deep shade here-about. The whole place looked as though it needed sunlight. When he felt clean and refreshed he began pulling at the rushes in the water, tugging until they came loose at the roots in great bundles. He laid them thriftily along the bank to dry, in a space he cleared. They'd be useful later.

The stream ran darkly muddy for a short time, roiled by the damage, and then he saw minnows darting, a great school of them. For worms provided by his ruthless disturbance? He stood watching the little fish while the water dripped from his body. That was when he saw the small duck, paddling along weakly and alone. He looked round for the rest of the brood, leaning to part the rushes on the farther bank. But there was no sign and no sound either, he realized, of hungry birds feeding. He had frightened all the marsh life into silence.

"I'll give you a home," he said to the duck, as he plucked it out of the water. It was very young, he saw, when he smoothed the beautiful greenish blue feathers, the first to appear after baby down. Mayhap it would divert Georgie for a few days, while the colony was still so unsettled.

It was time to go back to the height and see what would be set out for breakfast. He used his white shirt with its frilled cuffs to finish drying himself, an awkward process with one hand, but he couldn't put the duck down. It might wander off and be worse in its orphaning on land than in the water, though presumably near to its home in the reeds. Besides, the thought of Georgie's eyes when he bestowed it made his hold the firmer on the forlorn bird.

He struggled in the same way with his dressing and was minded of shirts by the wet one he carried and he began to sing, softly, when he started up the path.

> *Can you make me a cambric shirt*
> *Without a seam or fine needlework?*
> *Then a teasalum, tasalum, templum.*

A PLANT FOR HEALING

He knew when he was near the top by the sounds he could hear, above his own voice. He had been away just long enough. The men were stirring. They had a fire going at the cooking place, by the smell of smoke and the crackle of dry wood. Mayhap they meant to make corn-porridge this morning. They would be the cooks. The women would prepare their own meal at the Indian camp.

The path came out very close to the spot where he and Nias had walked and talked the night before. It was screened so well by a thick clump of bushes and young trees that anyone might have missed it, an he had been in a hurry at dawn time and had plunged down hill any fashion.

As he stepped into full view of the camp, bracing himself for gibes about his love of bathing and the foolish figure he must make, carrying a wet shirt, a bunch of watercress and a struggling, barely month-old duckling, he was welcomed with relief.

Dion Harvie rushed toward him, grasped his arm and urged him to the campfire. "Humphrey, where have you been? Nias is . . . he was the only one didn't rouse . . . he doesn't speak. You'll have to tell Mistress Dare."

Several of the men were kneeling beside Nias, still wrapped in his great cape. Humphrey's knees shook. Did they mean Nias was dead? But how could that be? He handed the duck to one, the shirt and watercress to others and knelt next to Roger Prat who was holding Nias's hand.

Lady of Roanoke

He looked at Humphrey and said, quietly, "No need to be affrighted, boy. Not yet. It's a fever of some kind. His body is very hot. But he shouldn't be left here. Shelter must be arranged."

Humphrey leaned closer and pressed Nias's neck under the ear, to see if he could rouse him. It was a trick learned from Manteo to use when there was danger afoot and silence precious.

Nias turned his head, opened his eyes and looked at them, vaguely at first, then he recognized Humphrey. "Ah lad," he said, weakly. "Up early for the planting? I thought to rest a bit longer. I'm so . . . tired." His voice trailed off and he slept again.

Humphrey rose, looked at Roger Prat, as if leaving him instead of Dion to see to Nias and said, "I'll get Mary," and was off, running toward the Indian village. No member of the tribe was ever ill long, after she dosed him. Could she do the same for Nias? What was wrong with him? True, he had complained of an aching head the night before and twice had seemed to lose the thread of their talk, but everybody was trail worn. Strange that only Nias should be ill.

The boy reasoned and worried as he ran and was so out of breath when he reached the first of the mat houses that he couldn't speak, and he didn't know which one was Mary's. He hadn't been taken round the village the day before. And where were the women of the colony? There, someone was up because smoke was spiraling from an early fire. That meant food. They'd all be rising presently, what matter if a little

A PLANT FOR HEALING

sooner than usual? If the old chief was angered, that would have to be set right afterward.

Humphrey took one more gasping breath, then he shouted, desperately, for Manteo and Mary.

They came. Everybody came, all frightened or curious. They poured out of the houses and from the woods where some of the young men were prowling in the dawn time as Humphrey had been, the colony women hurrying more than the rest for recognizing his voice.

What was toward? What did Humphrey mean, scaring everyone? Was he hurt?

"No, I want medicine for Nias. He's bad off. Mary, please come." He waved the others away. "I didn't know which house," he apologized, and Manteo turned and explained to his relatives why Humphrey had come and what the noise meant.

"See to the children, please, Betsey," said Eleanor to her helper, and started along the path to the camp without waiting for the others, who, sensibly, were asking Humphrey what the illness was, which Manteo patiently explained to his mother. She nodded, sent a woman scurrying to her house for a small earthen bowl which was brought, and then she was ready.

On the path as he followed the two Indians, Humphrey felt a small hand thrust into his and looked down and there was Georgie, his eyes as big as plums. "Is Nias going to be dead, the way my father was? Is he, Humphrey? But you'll take care of us, won't you?"

Humphrey stopped and knelt on one knee to bring

his face to a level with the little boy's and looked at him earnestly. This child had already seen too much trouble. What could he say to steady him?

"You're up a little early this morning, aren't you?"

"It was you waked me, Humphrey, when you shouted. I was scared."

"I had to shout, because I didn't know which house was Mary's. Nias is not well. He has a fever, and Mary knows how to take care of it. That's why I wanted her right quickly. Why are you here, Georgie?"

"I . . . I like to be by you, Humphrey, when I'm scared."

"And what about Johnnie Prat? Wasn't he frightened, too? You promised me you'd look after him."

"He's asleep," said Georgie. "Can't I go with you? Please, Humphrey."

"And what good will that do?"

"I . . . I want to see Nias. Then I can tell you if he's dead. I could. I saw my father. Let me come."

Humphrey hesitated, then he remembered the duck. If the man he had given charge of it had kept his wits, the bird might still be there to give to Georgie. It might help him forget about dead people.

For a wild moment, he wished that Sir Walter Raleigh had been content to serve his Queen at home instead of starting colonies for her. Then this child and the others who would grow up here, might have had less to grieve them. Or would they? Did things happen anyway to some people, no matter where they lived?

He stood up and said, "Come along, then, but we

shan't need you to tell us about Nias. He's going to
be well."

The delay with Georgie meant that they met the
little group of men bringing Nias to the Indian village,
where Mary had asked them to carry him. She led
them, still clutching her bowl. It held something
creamy-white, thick and greasy looking.

Eleanor was walking by Nias's head, and holding
one of his hands. He seemed asleep, still. She spoke to
Humphrey, said that Roger Prat was going to nurse
him with her. She looked frightened, but her voice was
brave and she was practical, too.

"Get your breakfast, Humphrey, and see that
Georgie has his. That will help Betsey."

It seemed strange to Humphrey that day that an
illness would bring about more spontaneous action than
anyone had thought possible in view of the disagree-
ment and argument which had preceded the vote to
build log houses.

One by one the six men Nias had deputed to help
with the planting came to their stripling leader after
breakfast and said they were ready to begin any time.
He had expected far different treatment from them, but
didn't show surprise. Instead, he spoke as he hoped
Nias would have done.

"Thank you, gentlemen. Have any of you dug or
planted before? No?" He grinned at their rueful faces.
"Then we will learn together. I haven't either, not in
a large field. I have only to find a piece of lost property. Then we shall see how we fare."

Lady of Roanoke

They watched him cross the green, followed by his faithful shadow and heard the natural, childish question.

"What have you lost, Humphrey?"

"You'll see, an I find it."

He spoke to one and another, meeting headshakes and grins until he came to the knot of men listening to Mark Bennet.

The carpenter was red of face, excited, but not angry. "The Dare house, first," he was insisting. "A mat one is no place for Nias to be ill in. Prat says he's afraid it is one of those long-lasting fevers. Up it goes, today. Ah, Humphrey, you want your shirt? It's just there, drying."

Humphrey had forgot his garment. It was more important that someone had found an extra doublet-lacing and sensibly looped it round the duck's neck and tied the ends to the same bush where the shirt was spread.

Georgie said, "You mean it's mine, Humphrey, to keep?"

"You'll have to take care of it yourself, and not let it bother Eleanor or Mistress Betsey."

"What does it eat?"

"Same as your goose did, Georgie," said Dion Harvie, reassuringly.

The ground in the fields was indeed hard and after the burning of the dried weeds, the first seemed to have baked the earth still more, just as Humphrey had felt

A PLANT FOR HEALING

it would. So he was agreeably surprised, when they broke through the caked surface, with the wooden spadelike hand implements the Indians used, to find some moisture beneath, and thus the promise of a crop was more hopeful. The ashes from the burning would feed the soil a little, another good omen.

Without a word said, some of the Indian women appeared when the land was ready, to show the awkward Englishmen how to plant corn—four kernels in a hill, and those about an inch apart, leaving enough room between the rows for the beans.

And when it was all done, a week's aching, backbreaking, unaccustomed labor, the waiting time began, for the first shoots to appear. The bean planting would come later, when the corn was high enough. They'd take only ten days to sprout up.

Humphrey was sorry, after a fashion, that it was finished. With a job to do, so tiring that he could scarcely keep awake long enough to eat his supper at night, he hadn't had time to worry about Nias. That had been left to others, and he sought Roger Prat after he had carefully collected and returned to the village all the borrowed implements: the seed baskets, the wooden spades, the water jugs and hole diggers.

The fever hadn't yet broken, but Roger was hopeful. "The man was worn out, more than we guessed," he remarked, thoughtfully, eyeing Humphrey for agreement.

"Worried some, too," said Humphrey, not telling why. "I can help now. Want me, for anything?"

Lady of Roanoke

"There's a plant I'd like to find," said Roger. "Harvie and Cooper will take a hand here so I can leave. It'd help Mistress Betsey if we take the children to the woods. They could play while I search."

Humphrey said, "Have to take them all, not just ours and Johnnie. What kind of plant?"

"Boneset, 'tis called," said Roger, "but I can't find out the Indian word and Mary doesn't recognize it from my description, though she must have some, dried. She will know it when she smells it. An infusion of the leaves will cause perspiration and it has a tonic quality, too. An we could break Nias's fever . . . Mary has made sassafras tea. 'Tis a good physic. But I want to try my idea, too."

Humphrey asked about the white stuff in the bowl. Roger laughed and wrinkled his nose. "Bear grease and other medicaments she uses. She rubs him with it. For the fever ache. It's good, but the smell, ah. . . . We keep as many mat openings uncovered as possible. An we find my plant, all may yet be well."

They discovered wild strawberries that afternoon, and located several nut trees, which they marked to visit later, when the harvest was ripe.

"Be sure that the Indians and the squirrels know where they are, too," said Roger, "but we'll get some of them."

He found his plant when he had almost given up hope, the white-flowered variety, and he exclaimed so excitedly about it that the surprised children, their mouths red with strawberry juice, forgot to ask ques-

A PLANT FOR HEALING

tions and stood watching him select the best of the
little patch and then protect it with a ring of brush so
it could be found again, easily.

"Now Nias will be well, and shortly, I hope," he
said with such satisfaction that Humphrey knew the
man had had doubts of Nias's recovery.

When they were ready to start homeward, Virginia said, "My foot hurts, Humphrey."

He took her up pickaback, thinking they ought to
have asked for one of Mary's little island horses for
the trip. But the child wasn't heavy and he felt glad
they hadn't borrowed. It was becoming an easy habit.
Some day that must change.

A NEW COLONIST

10

Humphrey Hall stood on a large block of stone near the cooking place the next morning, teetering back and forth because it was uneven and poorly balanced, in pleasurable indecision as to what he would do next. It was going to be a beautiful summer day and he had several choices of occupation, now that the corn crop was planted for good or ill.

He could ask Mark Bennet for a job.

He could collect the children and keep them from bothering other people. Someone should, until the school was started.

He could slip away from everybody and go down

to the stream to begin work on the pool he meant to
have.

He could find Eleanor and see if she had need of
him.

But he had too wide a selection to decide in a
hurry and there seemed plenty of time. The smell of
breakfast, just over—venison broiled over the coals of
the open hearth—was still rich in the cool air.

He looked around the busy scene and thought
whimsically that Mark Bennet could be trying to make
a shirt without a needle. A full week ago he had insisted on starting Nias's house that very day, but it was
still not begun, though there was a rumor that the
work had again been appointed, for this morning.

Nothing was done, so far, because they'd had to
root out the tree stumps that dotted the green. The Indians' method of burning out the roots first was slow,
but it worked, and now there were smooth bare spots
in the grass where the huge trees had been. Loose stones
for foundation outlined the shape of the new dwellings.

Nias's was to face the green at the end between
the open hearth and the path to the Indian village, and
directly opposite on the south side would be the Rectory. The Long House, following Roger Prat's idea,
would be in the middle, in easy reach of every house,
on the east side.

Humphrey tried to imagine what his new home
would look like, when finished. The first room, where
one entered, seemed suspiciously large, compared to
what they'd had at Roanoke or to others planned here.

Lady of Roanoke

And there were to be three rooms behind it, from the look of the design, a really sizeable house. Did Eleanor know? Nias wouldn't like it, to live in a better one than any other in the colony.

Was Mark taking advantage of Nias's illness and making that front room larger so the school could meet in it? That had been in his mind, for the school to be held in one of the houses.

Humphrey glanced uneasily toward the spot where the Long House was to be and was much relieved to see that it didn't look smaller than was meant in the beginning, though he hadn't seen Thomas Warner's measurements. For that matter, Nias's could be deceptive, too, and when finished that front room might not seem so large.

But if it was Mark's idea to put the school there and he had appealed to the Patentees to see it his way, how could Nias bear the chatter and confusion of the children's coming and going? He was better off, quieter, under the mat-hung framework in the Indian village.

Humphrey was annoyed with himself to question everything Mark Bennet did, but all the man's actions since their leaving Roanoke warranted it. Yet, who was he to take it on himself to run to one or another of the Patentees and say it must be stopped, that Nias wouldn't want a pretentious house, nor that big room? He'd be as blameworthy as Mark, an he did. Neither was it anything he could worry Eleanor about.

While he still teetered, unable to decide anything, he was the unbidden witness of a small drama that once more gave the women their way, this time unopposed by Mark Bennet.

First, up the path from the village came two of the colony women, hurrying, Margery Harvie and Mistress Betsey, who carried William and led Virginia by the hand. Behind them Jane Berry and Joan Warner panted along. Something was afoot.

As if on signal, the rector came out of the woods back of the cooking place, in his vestments, ready for a service. Meaning to bless the foundations of the new houses? It looked that way.

Mark Bennet left the men he'd been haranguing near the piles of logs and came rushing over and met the rector and the women at the very spot which in time would be the Dares' front door.

And there was Humphrey on his stone not six feet away.

But the succeeding gabble was hard to sort out, even that close by, so he jumped down and edged nearer to hear what was going on and he met the rest of the children, swarming after the women. Johnnie Prat clutched the duck.

"Where's . . . ?" Georgie began, and answered his own question when he saw Virginia. He jerked away from Humphrey's attempted restraint and stood importantly holding the little girl's hand. She tried to pull it away, with no help from Betsey Glane who was talking as hard as the rest.

It was John Brooke who got some order out of the hubbub, and then Humphrey, and anyone else who cared to, could hear that the women had decided to have stone floors in every house and Master Bennet wasn't to stir one log until he had done something to that end.

"We had all we wanted of dirt floors on Roanoke. We never thought of stones until this morning when we heard about raising the Dares' house. Mistress Dare would come and second the plan, an she were free to, but you know her situation."

Margery Harvie looked at Mark, belligerently, though he hadn't said a word. "With all the stone that's about and all the help you've got, it'll be easy. Not one of you but will be glad of the day, when the frost comes. We'll be weaving the mats to be warm under-foot. We're learning. Weaving and Coree talk and Mary and the others some English, and what will make purple and what pink in the dye pot. They find it in plants in the woods. Have the men learned so much? I venture not."

She included her own husband in the sweeping glance she gave the audience, which had now gathered, camp strong, around the group of women with Mark and the rector.

"Needn't scold me," said Mark. "I ain't said no."

"Nor yet yes," said Jane Berry.

Mark said, "Got no choice, have I?"

But Jane had turned to her husband. "Henry, we want stone floors and we mean to have the same. Dressin' the pieces ourselves wouldn't be too much to do to have good solid underfooting."

A NEW COLONIST

Henry said, "I forbid you, Jane. You'll not smooth any stones with colony tools. You'd have'm ruined in no time a-tall. Ours will have to last as long as ever we can make them do. Just think about that."

"Then, please, you get to fixin' the stones. I'll have nothin' less."

Mark said, "If you'd all quieten a bit, so's rector sir can bless the stones that will be, then we could begin. Can't put any kind of floor in until foundation is laid."

The desired hush fell, then, and the prayer was made and the women departed, happily, without one backward look, knowing their point was won. Humphrey found his choice of occupation made for him, because the children stayed behind.

He heard Mark say to John Brooke, "I do say, rector sir, ours is the termagantenest women I ever heard tell of, even back in England. Let one get an idea and they all buzz like bees in swarm. Will we ever please'm, ideas comin' one a minute?"

For once Mark wasn't angry, only puzzled, and he looked at the rector in genuine surprise when he laughed and said, "The trouble with us, Mark, you and me, is that we aren't married. I think somewhat of understanding of the female comes with that."

That did it. Mark's face got red as fire. "You ever tried askin' one of'm? Takes two to make a marriage." He walked away without excusing himself, and went back to his log piles and the men who'd have to begin dressing more stones.

Humphrey looked at the young brood waiting to be entertained. Six little boys and one small girl. There'd been some fighting of sorts. Robbie Ellis had a black eye. And one in the count was missing. "Where's Little Amby?" he asked.

Georgie said, wide-eyed, "He didn't come."

"Where's my dog?"

"Lion's tied up. Mistress Glane said . . ."

Humphrey jerked a thumb toward the mat houses. "Get him," he ordered. "Get them both, and hurry. I've got an idea you'll like."

He sat on the grass to wait and Virginia climbed onto his shoulders, promptly. "Carry me, Humphrey?"

"You don't know where we are going."

"But I'm a girl. I don't want to walk. My foot hurts."

He thought, idly, she was always complaining about her feet. Speak to Eleanor, mayhap. Put her in moccasins instead of those clumsy leather shoes. He was watching the woods and when the brush collectors appeared he whistled shrilly and John and Billy heard and came running, after dumping their loads.

"Help me?" he asked, including the children in his gesture. "These are to be minded, and two more and the dog, and I want to clear us out a pool in the stream below. Work, but it's worth it. If any fall in, I'll need some older folks along to help pull them out." He winked at the boys and they grinned.

"Older folks, Humphrey?" said Billy. "You couldn't say better. We're almost-fourteens. We can pack out more wood, after noon meal."

A NEW COLONIST

Little Amby was fat, and he came toiling along the path, holding Georgie's hand and beaming. He wore a clean shirt. He'd had to wait for it to dry and cried because he was left behind. He carried his basket. "My mother said, mayhap we'll find something to put in it."

They had a glorious, sloppy wet morning by the stream. Little Amby was the only clean child who returned motherward or otherwise at noon time. That was because Humphrey had removed the splendid shirt and hung it on a bush so that the little boy might have a good time with the rest. More rushes were uprooted and the little duck escaped Johnnie Prat's hands and was no more seen. They filled the basket with fresh watercress and picked a bunch of wild blue lilies for the women's mat house. The big boys heaved and tugged at stones and the pool began to take shape. No one wanted to leave when it was time to climb by the winding path to the camp.

That afternoon Humphrey ventured to offer a turn at sitting by Ananias and free someone else for the building.

Though Mary and Roger Prat and Eleanor had tended him faithfully, the patient's slow progress was discouraging. The constant sponging helped reduce the bear grease odor as well as the fever but it rose again at night.

Nias was quiet much of the time but there were moments when he rolled and muttered and beat the mats he lay upon with his feeble fists, calling for Eleanor. One of the worst of these times happened when Humphrey had been there a scant half hour. Nias tried to get out of bed in his agitation, and had to be held back, forcibly. Then Roger held the bowl of infusion for him to drink and when the sweat began to roll, they sponged again and put on a clean night rail.

Humphrey was shocked, when the muttering began, to hear quiet, dignified Ananias Dare say, earnestly, "Eleanor, we mustn't have any more children . . . mumble, mumble . . . they will . . . only . . . die. Hide William! Keep him safe!"

Roger soothed and massaged in vain. Nias tossed away from the gentle hands and talked on.

"Why doesn't your father come? When he does . . . mumble . . . an he does, Eleanor . . . go home. We'll all go. Oh, when will Bennet and Warn . . . Warner realize we'll never . . . Eleanor, forgive . . . I shouldn't have brought you . . ."

The tired voice dulled and Nias slept again.

Humphrey met Roger's eyes across the bed and the man said, sorrowfully, "Now, you know. With this burden on his mind, how can he get well?"

"I've known, since the second day on the trail," said Humphrey, steadily, "that there were some things people might worry about. Eleanor told me. I think . . ."—no need to tell Roger Prat why he thought it—"that even if Governor White comes back, some time, he'll never find us. We aren't a true colony now. Nias was worrying to me the night before he . . . oh, Roger, what will we *do*, if Nias should . . ."

A NEW COLONIST

"Nay, lad, do not dwell on it. And we *are* a colony as long as we don't admit anything different to each other and most particularly not to the Indians. For the children's sake, we must act as a colony would. And who shall say that the Governor will not return? There are some, Humphrey, who still believe that he will and shall yet find us. It's to please them that an extra large room is to be built in Nias's house. The Governor's room."

Humphrey said, "They have much faith," and did not let Roger Prat know how grateful he was for that piece of news.

Roger took up his bowl, preparing to sponge Nias again. "Tomorrow," he said, "an Manteo's snares yield a partridge or two, Eleanor will make broth for Nias. We'll try everything we know. And there'll be another patient shortly, for someone to look after. Mistress Viccars is near her time, so they tell me."

Humphrey groaned. "Oh the poor lady. I'd forgot about her. It seems . . ."

"Yes, lad," Roger urged.

"So many things to worry us, all the time."

"But that's life," said the older man. "It would be the same in England, had we never come to the New World. Things go along, then this frets and that bothers and something else turns out the wrong way. Man is not free to order his world, to make it run smoothly all the time. We, here, only seem to have it a little harder because we have less to do with, is all. And we're learning, Humphrey, I to use my hands in ways

Lady of Roanoke

I never knew in England. And you can't deny, lad, that you . . ."

Humphrey said, "I know, sir. I wouldn't have it any different, for myself. It's the children." He frowned. "The school should begin, to keep them safely all in one place for part of the day. Now they're running wild, and it's going to be harder to gather them in, later. They should have something of their own to do. Today the women asked Mark for stone floors in all the houses. Stone, Roger, that needs to be heaved out and cut and smoothed and fitted. I don't know how much that will delay commencing the building. I mind it because I'd thought if we could move Nias into his own house he might sense through the fever that we were going a little forward and it'd help him get better. If only we could reason with him . . ."

Roger nodded and considered, while he smoothed his beard. "I'll speak to Warner," he said, finally, "when I get opportunity. Nias was talking about the school that same night, when he spoke to you last. He couldn't get to sleep after we lay down. There are eight of us Patentees to share the thinking, when he directs. He shouldn't have kept so much to himself, but I doubt not, many here have had thoughts they didn't dare bring out."

Humphrey grinned. "The women have no like fears. They speak their mind and ask for stone floors. They're all making mats against the time they'll each be in a house to spread them around. And they seem

to be learning the Coree tongue and teaching ours to the
Indian women while they weave."

He stopped and listened and gestured outside,
where shrill little voices could be heard in a fierce dispute. "Hear them? One black eye already doesn't seem
enough. And the little Lady of Roanoke right in the
middle and getting her own way because she's the only
girl. They all give in to her, from Tommy Archard
down. He's the oldest. It isn't right, Roger. The children have the most need of all."

Roger said, apologetically, "It's true, Humphrey,
and I'm afraid I've left my Johnnie too much to
Mistress Dare's care, this while."

Humphrey said, gruffly, because he was so moved
by the man's humility, when he had proved himself to
be a truly great person, "There's no blame to that, sir.
She takes in all the strays, does Mistress Dare. Haven't
you seen? Georgie and me, for two. Same as on
Roanoke. And Johnnie is no trouble. Georgie keeps him
in sight."

Roger Prat looked relieved. "I didn't know that.
I've been uneasy, a little."

And then Dion Harvie came, to take his turn beside Nias, and Humphrey was free. He stopped at the
site of the Dares' house and asked if he could help but
Mark gave him a disgusted look and shook his head,
so he went on down to the pool, to work off some of
his worries.

He stood a moment on the bank of the little stream
to look at the morning's work. It wouldn't take long to

have it clean and clear. An they could shape the bed, so to deepen it that the flow became less sluggish, the bad odor would disappear. It was already less noticeable.

It took three days to prepare enough stones for the floors of the Dares' house and then it began to rise steadily, with all hands assembled, and Humphrey was grudgingly allowed to help, because he was needed. His assignment was definite.

"Here's Humphrey Hall. His *back's* strong." Implying that his mind might not be?

Humphrey couldn't understand why Mark was still so surly or sarcastic when he had to speak to him directly.

Now Mark added, "You see to the mortar-mixing, Humphrey, and mind you keep it moving. We'll need a lot."

It was the most menial job of all, mixing mud and sand to chink the logs. It didn't require much but strength and enduring application. Every job was needed, all parts of a whole, to get Nias's house built, as fast as possible.

But work hard as they did, it took a full week to raise that house, log by log and room by room, and roof it on the eighth day, with fine cedar shingles shaped by the tools brought from England.

No one in Humphrey's hearing had ever worried aloud how long those good edges and solidly set handles would last. But they must know that you could sharpen an adz, a carpenter's double one, or the kind used on ships—and the men had both—or anything you cut with, just so often, and then the metal wore down and there was nothing left to whet. Of course, after the houses were built, there wouldn't be as much wear on tools, except to cut fireplace wood and make odd repairs. Oh, but there'd have to be some furniture made. The spinning wheel, cradle, anvil and various family chests were all the heavy things they had been able to bring from Roanoke.

On the morning the Dares' house was finished, the women of the colony who were most experienced rose before dawn to help Elizabeth Viccars bear her daughter Ann, and Little Amby cried all day at intervals because he had wanted a brother.

Girls weren't any good, he said, and before anyone could prevent her, Virginia gave him a good hard slap for his opinion, which only made the poor little boy roar louder.

Virginia herself was three years old that day and no one guessed immediately that the slapping was meant for the new baby who had dared to be born a girl and on *her* birthday.

All the little boys took poor Amby's part for once and my Lady of Roanoke went sobbing to Humphrey, who suspected what might be wrong but did not probe.

A ride on one of Mary's Barbarys might help, he thought, anxiously hoping for diversion. It did help, for a few hours. The later consequences of his idea lasted longer.

THOMAS WARNER SPEAKS HIS MIND

11

The whole colony benefited in one way and another by Robbie Ellis's black eye, sustained a couple of days before the Dare house was begun, though Humphrey hoped that the children would never know what happened to Mark Bennet on account of it. The story came to him in roundabout fashion and wasn't meant to be common knowledge.

Building that first colony house pushed everything else out of the Patentees' minds for the time it took, but Robbie's eye helped indirectly thereafter to get the school under way.

When the effort was over and the Dare family was

moved in, the master carpenter wisely eased the pressure which had lasted so long and announced a holiday. It was done, though, in a patronizing way which had been increasing, toward the men, ever since their coming from Roanoke. It spoiled the pleasant prospect of change, even for a day, from their long routine of hard work. Mark had been a shipyard carpenter at Brixham before coming to Roanoke, the men knew, yet he talked to them as a hard-tempered squire might, to yeoman labor.

There were exclamations, raised eyebrows, winks and only a few muttered oaths. They let it pass because a free day meant a swim in Humphrey's partly finished pool, or a visit to their old friends in the Indian village—even a little extra sleep before starting the next house.

Thomas Ellis, widower, also renewed association with his young Robbie aged ten years, and saw the lingering traces of that black eye.

At supper Mark heard the first rumbles of the man's complaints and joined the group he was eating with, to hear the better, which made Thomas thereupon address him directly.

"Neglect, that's what I call it," said the excited father. " 'Tis purely natural for young sprouts to fight. That ain't my worry now. I say, had somebody put somethin' on my boy's eye right away, he needn't have worn a bandage long as he did. Might have hurt himself far worse, seein' only half. Mark Bennet, an I have to stop work, to tend the boy myself . . ."

Lady of Roanoke

He didn't need to finish his threat because Mark was walking away fast, bent on finding Thomas Warner, his fellow committee-man for houses. It didn't matter that Robbie's eye was now well.

Thomas Warner had finished his meal, was wiping his knife before putting it away in the case he carried in his doublet, and he stepped away reluctantly, out of other mens' hearing, at Mark's gesture, to hear his story.

"Why didn't the women take care of Robbie? Didn't belong to any of'm, was that it, so they let'm alone? Then neglect it was, just as the boy's father thinks."

"Well, now, Mark, are you sure you know the whole story?"

"All I got to say is, we have to be roofed by frost, the whole colony, and I can't have the children causin' delay, whole story or not. A main nuisance, all of'm, and quarrelsome. If the fathers get upset and won't work, how will the houses get up? Had we a school, the shavers'd be controlled in some part. Humphrey Hall helps with'm all he can, but . . ." he stopped because the Oxford man was staring at him, plainly astonished.

"*Praise?* For Humphrey?"

Mark got red, but went on, defiantly, adding a sting, " 'Bout all he *is* good for, now that the planting is done."

"And mixing mud for chinking," Thomas reminded him.

"Well . . . well . . . somebody had to do that."

THOMAS WARNER SPEAKS HIS MIND

"And he did it right smartly, smooth, no stones in it, as he does everything he tries," said Humphrey's advocate, sternly, "though I doubt not you hoped for complaint from him, or failure. You gave him that job on purpose. It was noticed. I was watching for one."

He stood a moment, quietly considering, while Mark sputtered incoherently. Was this the time to settle everything with the cocky carpenter? Would there ever be a better? What risk? He himself had had enough of the man's overbearing, patronizing manner. Would the Patentees back him? They might think that he was taking a lot for granted, to give the man a set-down. No, from the talk going about, he didn't think they'd mind.

When Mark stopped for breath, his fellow committeeman said, "The fact is, Bennet, you're mean. Except for Nias Dare falling ill, I doubt not the Patentees would've had you before them, for your bad grace."

Mark said, "Ho-ho!" scornfully.

"Bad grace," Thomas repeated. "All you've won by it is to make yourself the butt of colony laughter—when we've had a moment to laugh about anything. Jealousy does not become any man, Bennet, and I'll hope this needs be said to you just once. Think on it."

"Why should I?"

"Because Humphrey Hall is the most alone person amongst us. There is no youth his own age, for companionship, and no girl in the colony he might marry. So, except he finds a comely Indian maid to wife, he may have a sorry future ahead. He hasn't realized it yet, but it's the only way he'll get that farm he wants—by marrying it. No one has the heart to tell him. That's been Manteo's purpose all along, some of us think. And you can be jealous of *him*, with that prospect? True he is a gentleman's son with a manor of his own in England. But he gave that up to come here and share alike with us, to do his part in establishing a colony. Why? Because he didn't care, young as he then was, for an easy life. He wanted to work with his hands, build something by his own skill."

Mark was studying his feet now, not meeting the steely Warner eye.

"You even tried to tell the Dares how *they* should live, by your insistence that Humphrey could have a pallet somewhere—he'd be fitted in—the families were *neighbors* in Yorkshire! That was more bad grace. What if they did want to continue, do want to, as they did on Roanoke, taking in two homeless boys as their own? That was not *your* concern, if anyone's. Oh, it was heard. Other people besides Nias Dare were listening when you offered your unasked-for arrangements."

Mark burst out, vehemently, "You ain't a Patentee, Warner. Forgettin', ain't you, you're only a colonist same as me? No call your talkin' this way. Patentees should think twice about havin' me up. I'm buildin'm houses, I am."

"We can act without the Patentees, an we must," said Thomas Warner, quietly, surer now that what he was saying would save trouble later. "An I would, I could tell you . . . I think I *will* tell you, Bennet, that it's been talked of, more than once, to hand you a gun, a blanket and journey-food and send you on your way to the coast. Then you could join those other colonists of ours who might still be waiting for an English ship to come along and take them home with all the gold they've found . . . if they're not all dead by this time."

Mark stared at him, unbelievingly, before he quavered, "Alone? You wouldn't!"

"It would be kinder, of course," the even, quiet voice went on, "to let you wait for Manteo's people when they make their trip to the ocean for fish next spring. You *could* go then. It depends on how you treat Humphrey Hall from now on and how you speak to the men. There are several good carpenters among them. I've noted who they are."

Then, without giving Mark further chance to bluster or argue, he changed his severe tone to a casual one.

"You may tell the men that the school has been discussed. Roger Prat came to me with it because Humphrey had been urging action—yes, Humphrey— but we were about to begin building Nias's house. Perhaps some classes should have been started sooner. But it has not been easy to make choice of first things, here. You know that well, man."

Thomas was turning away, glad to have the unpleasantness finished, when he thought of one more thing. He looked around and saw Mark still standing where he had left him, with a blank look on his face. He said, "Only you and I need know of this conversa-

Lady of Roanoke

tion, Bennet. Take another well-meant hint. Don't go scolding the women for neglecting Robbie Ellis's eye— oh, I know what stirred this up, I heard the father scolding—the mothers are doing very well for all the children, most of us think, under great hardship."

It was Humphrey who found out the whole circumstance about the eye, from the beginning of the fight to the bandage and the eventual cure, with Georgie Howe to tell him the tale.

"Mary sent Felicity and one of the big girls with Robbie and me to the woods to look for a plant. She has some dried in a bag, but she said now is the fresh time and if we helped to find it, maybe we wouldn't fight any more."

"What does the plant look like?"

"It's this high . . ." Georgie measured what would be a tall one . . . "but it isn't a bush. The leaves are all together at the bottom and there's a long stem with bright yellow flowers on top."

"And . . .?"

"We picked the flowers and some leaves and took them to Mary and she boiled them in a pot and brown juice was made with a nice smell. I put it on Robbie's eye every day with a piece of old shirt, and the black went away. Can I go and play now, Humphrey?"

"After you've told me the rest. You started at the end, I think."

Georgie looked at his feet. "Do I have to tell?

We . . . Robbie and I . . . said we wouldn't fight any more."

"Mayhap, not until the next time," said Humphrey, gravely. He sighed heavily to show he was much concerned about fighting. "It's so easy," he added.

Georgie propped his elbows on Humphrey's knee and looked up at him with a glowing face, and the blue eyes danced. "Then you used to fight, too," he crowed, "you know all about it."

"Not everything, quite yet, about this one fight. I'm waiting to hear. Not to tell anyone. Just to think about."

Georgie removed himself nimbly from Humphrey's reach, ready to scamper, if what he said wasn't agreeable. "Robbie likes . . ." he began haltingly, ". . . he's two years older than me, Humphrey, he's ten, and he gives Virginia rides on his back. Oh, he's quite strong. It's because she says her foot hurts. Humphrey, I don't think it does, she just wants rides. So, we were . . . *do* I have to tell?"

Humphrey thought he could now guess what might be coming. He said, talking stiffly, to keep laughter down, which would only dismay poor Georgie, "I . . . think, yes . . . it might . . . be a very good idea." Then, more easily, "I have promised, you remember, that I wouldn't tell anyone. An you like, come close and you may whisper it."

So Georgie stood at his knee again and said, very low, "Robbie said that Virginia likes him better than me, so I . . . I hit him."

"Good man!" said Humphrey, "for telling me," he added, hastily. "Now I will say something. If I ever catch Virginia riding on anyone's back but mine, she will get a sound spanking . . . from me."

The big eyes opened wider. "She will, Humphrey?"

"She will. If you like, you may tell that to all the other children. Now, run off, I want to think. And no more fights."

The Patentees held a hasty meeting next day, perching on the stones that outlined their Long House, and invited the rector and Humphrey to sit with them, in sight of the whole colony, to talk over starting the school. Roger Prat, looking worn, arrived last and sat by Humphrey.

"How does Nias fare?"

They all asked it and Roger said, quietly, that he was responding to the change as they had hoped he might. "He lies in the big room and he will get well now, I think."

Had he doubted it, then? They looked at each other, uneasily, and no one asked that question.

Dion Harvie presided in Nias's place. He said, "We needn't linger this morning. Everyone—at least those who have paid it some mind—feels that the children should be set to learning. We have delayed overlong and how to go about it is more the worry now. Rector, sir, have you an idea?"

"The catechism," said John Brooke, promptly. "That, above everything, for a start."

"Good for everyone, any time," said Chris Cooper, heartily, "but for other learning, ages make a difference. Ought to start with that, mayhap. How old are the children?"

Dion glanced around and remarked, "Only two fathers here."

He raised his eyebrows at them, inquiringly, and John Sampson said, "My John will be fourteen in November."

Roger Prat said, "My Johnnie is six, just."

"Mayhap you know the others, Humphrey," Dion urged. "You are closest to all the children."

Humphrey thought a moment, frowning. "Billy Wythers is next to John Sampson. They both like to say they're almost-fourteens. Billy is George Martyn's nephew. Robbie Ellis is ten. He's the one that got the black eye." The men chuckled. "Then we have three Thomases. I'm one of them, the Thomas Humfrey on the list. That's the way I applied to Sir Walter." He grinned. "Tommy Archard is about nine, I think. Georgie Howe comes next, he's eight. The third Thomas, name of Smart, is Billy's cousin, and six years old. Little Amby Viccars won't be six for several months. Six little boys, three big ones and a little girl, if we have Virginia. Though only three, it'd help her mother if she comes to the class."

Dion nodded and said, "Thank you, boy," and Chris Cooper remarked, "He does know them. No easy thing to decide what they should learn. Who's to do the teaching?"

No one had an idea, and Dion looked at the rector who shook his head.

After that silence, Humphrey ventured. "D'you want me to say what Nias had in mind? He spoke to me of school that last night before he was seized of the fever."

"Of course, boy, tell it," said Dion.

"He hoped Master Warner would teach numbers . . . all the sums. And there'd be Tom-the-Lute for singing. Roger Prat knows plants. He can show them how to keep away from hurtful things in the woods. Then there's Latin." Humphrey glanced at the rector. "I . . . I'd like to go on with mine, even if no other is apt for it. I am ready to start Virgil, an I may. That's all, sirs."

"And plenty," said Dion, briskly.

Roger Prat spoke, a little diffidently, as always. "You might . . ." he hesitated ". . . I've found that there is . . . that is to say, Mistress Mannering taught at a dance school at home and she has had experience in giving young ladies deportment. Mayhap she could see to Virginia and the six-year-olds. You could ask her."

"Splendid!" said Dion. "The head can act on it." He turned to John Brooke. "Rector, sir, you will be that one? Our headmaster? An that is decided, we can leave the rest in your hands and end the waiting."

"Oh, no, Harvie, it's not to be thought of. I shouldn't have two responsible jobs. With an Oxford scholar among us, there can't be any doubt about our don. Thomas Warner it must be, an he consents."

Dion looked relieved to have that much assured,

put the vote, and it was left to the rector to talk to Warner, the Oxford man.

"Mark Bennet won't like us taking Warner for the school," said Roger Bayly, as they separated, "another good workman from the houses and his committee-man."

John Sampson was naturally slow-spoken, expressing himself adequately for the most part with grins and nods or frowns. But now he said, sternly, "He can't have it his way all the time. He wanted a school to get the children from under foot. They weren't under his. Never saw one of them bother him. So we'll pay him no heed. He has said quite enough to everyone already on any matter."

A BARBARY PONY

12

The first week of school was not a marked success.

Thomas Warner was indeed a scholar and he was a patient and kind man, but he knew the intricacies of his own art, its theories and practical use, far better than the way to make it interesting to a group of boys whose attention strayed.

How could they help it, with the school meeting out of doors and a new house going up directly across the green, especially when several fathers were in sight? Which was the faster workman, or more skilled?

There was no difficulty about the catechism with which each day began.

A BARBARY PONY

Who made you?
God.

And on, in unison, glibly, or skipping syllables to the end of that day's lesson, in the varying trebles of the little boys and the beginning uncertainty of tone of the two older ones, as a vague obbligato.

The rector was pleased and took a different question to expound every morning.

But afterward, when Little Amby and Virginia were led away by Mistress Mannering to follow the flight of a butterfly or go down the slope to play beside the stream, the others wriggled and twisted to get a better view of the way the next log was settling into place, and gave all wrong answers to poor Thomas Warner until he was ready to throw his book at them.

Humphrey looked on and was troubled. The children needed something to hold in their hands. He had had paper and pens at Gilling and books and a desk to put them in. Here there was nothing. No one in the colony seemed to have thought of any kind of supply for a school when they packed their chests in England. Had they expected their children to grow up dullards? They could think of geese and cows and clothing, had brought a cradle and a spinning wheel and an anvil. At least Henry Berry could be excused of blame. He wasn't married, then. But why hadn't the rest brought a few books?

He said as much to the rector, who had brought one old horn book, with an alphabet in plain and capital letters, which the children could copy, an they had

Lady of Roanoke

the means. Learning their letters would be something. John Brooke shook his head, when Humphrey asked why he had brought it.

"It was there, on my shelf, so I packed it when the letter came from Sir Walter to say they'd be glad to have me on the expedition."

The two were talking by the hearth in Eleanor Dare's kitchen, after Betsey's good supper and Humphrey's first attempt at Virgil.

The boy thought wryly of the list he had been given—the requirements of a gentleman colonist, because they hadn't known he was a youth of fourteen—after he had secretly sent in his application to sail. Books were not mentioned but he had brought a few.

He watched John Brooke prepare to smoke the dried plant the Indians called *oppowoc*, in a clay pipe, tamping the fibers down well, to make a good drawing. It had constantly to be relighted and Humphrey kept a live coal ready for the necessity, holding it with a crude pincers Henry Berry had made.

Mistress Betsey would not leave them until she had Humphrey's earnest promise to bank the fire well, when his lesson was done. She was as thoroughgoing and earnest as Jane Berry had been. Or was it that she was growing to like rector sir? He came often to meals, but there always seemed a good reason, as this evening. It would be something to watch for, if another romance was afoot.

No one could blame Betsey or Eleanor for house pride. In a short time the two women had made the kitchen a family gathering room by the small arts of female practice which would always puzzle him, Humphrey decided. One could forget the bare logs— no plastering inside with the mud mixture until all the houses were up, only fair. One of Eleanor's chests stood against the inner wall. A heavy silver basin, brought from Yorkshire, and large enough to hold a great quantity of stew, stood upon it.

A tall, narrow jug, gift from Mary and filled with blue marsh lilies, stood on the floor in the corner by the door which led to the front room.

The mats, which all the seventeen had boasted of, covered a part of the stone floor. They were thick and soft to sit on, until the carpenters could begin making furniture. Some of the rushes they used had been colored to make a red warp, very pleasing.

The rector pointed to them with the stem of his pipe. "They get that bright color from *puccoon* juice, they tell me. When the ink powder I brought runs out, I shall have to resort to some such source for substitute. H'm! Well, Humphrey, this school matter seems to sit heavily on your young shoulders. Let it be, boy. You must not know that a number of the present adult company here cannot even write their names."

Humphrey gaped, horrified, because he had had no reason to note that lack. He thumped the hearthstone with his fist. "That I will not have for Georgie, nor for Virginia. Nias won't, either, when he comes to his good senses."

The rector tapped out his pipe, which meant he

was leaving. "They will learn," he said, confidently. "Right now everything looks distressful, because we are in the greenwood and not all are roofed. It is a choice between one bad thing and a worse. It helps everyone, even the children themselves, though they do not think so, to have a semblance of school for part of the day. When Nias is better, we may have the Governor's room. 'Tis that or stay out of doors, because I understand Bennet means to build the Long House last. He is right, though he gets his way so ungraciously—I'm sorry for the man—the people should have shelter, first. But you need not take on the worries of middle age, Humphrey, before you have enjoyed your youth. You are a great help to Mistress Dare, just because you are here. That's responsibility enough for one lad. Do twenty lines for me, tomorrow. Good night, boy!"

It was one thing, Humphrey reflected, to be told not to worry, and another, indeed, to make your mind blank. His own was like a copybook, heavily written, even underscored if something needed remedy.

His inner voice said, "How would you teach, an you had the doing?"

The way I was taught in dame school, with stories and the numbers and letters in, without my knowing it, he thought. But he couldn't picture Thomas Warner as a teller of tales, anywhere. The rector, only possibly.

Humphrey smiled at the good man's idea that the wriggling and confusion would stop when the school moved indoors. As a bachelor he was not used to children and Thomas Warner, though married, was not a parent. The smile became a chuckle in the dark, choked back for fear of waking Georgie on the pallet next him. He himself knew the children better than anyone except their mothers because they were with him so much. Somehow he must find the way to help them learn their letters, by copying the shapes from the rector's horn covered chart, which he had known as *The Absey Book*, when he was a child in Yorkshire.

It was only after he decided to see Manteo the next day about the school that he could think of his own private worry. Virgil's *Aeneid* wasn't going to be easy. He was mumbling *Of arms and a hero I sing* when sleep shut down.

He met Manteo in almost the exact middle of the path between the two settlements the next morning, when catechism was over.

The young Indian was carrying a small, squirming black dog. He said, "You told Georgie to say that the dog could come back when the house shall be ready." The deep humor gleam was in his eyes.

Humphrey was dismayed. He stood stroking the little black head and the puppy struggled to reach his face with a too-ready tongue. What was he to do? He had completely forgot the children's need for pets, in his distress about Nias and later, on account of their school. It was strange, though, that Georgie had not reminded him.

Manteo thought he was frowning at the little dog. "This is not the same one," he explained. "It is not . . . how do you say the female? Not what the other black one was."

Humphrey grinned and gathered in the little black

Lady of Roanoke

fellow, and he settled contentedly into the crook of his arm. All little dogs did. It was the way he had carried Lion home from the Corees' island, when Mary made him her gift.

Manteo said, "There is a lamb now, born out of season, and the ewe died. It is too young for a pet, but the children come over every day to look at all the animals and . . ."

Humphrey asked, briskly, "Does our little Lady of Roanoke know she is to have the lamb?"

Manteo shook his head.

"I thought it would not come until the *budding of spring*. Her father hoped we'd have a place then. Now I'm not sure . . ."

"He is not more well, then? He has not spoken yet?"

"Nay, Manteo, but he will. We see a betterment each day."

The Indian nodded. "That is the way of those fevers. Then one day he will open his eyes and know where he is and will speak . . ." Manteo imitated the lightness and the weakness they could expect in the tone ". . . and he will have a great hunger. That is when I must set many snares for the little birds and squirrels. . . . But it is more than about the lamb or the puppy that I am here."

"Then we will talk to Mistress Dare. Come."

They skulked through the woods beside the path and approached the Dares' back door out of sight of the green, but before Humphrey could call Eleanor,

A BARBARY PONY

Manteo said, "It is better for you to know what I'm come to say before we tell the White Doe. The little Lady of Roanoke does not want the lamb. She talks only of a pony. My sisters or the others let her ride every day. Now my mother wants to give her one, but she sent me to talk."

Humphrey was shocked. "The fault is mine, Manteo. When I first put her up, on the trail, I thought only of present need. She complained that her foot hurt. And another time, when the little boys scolded her, it was my way of comfort."

The gleam in Manteo's eyes deepened and he shook his head. "The foot, my brother, does not hurt. When a woman-child wants a thing, very much, she knows how to get it."

"But Manteo, the little Lady is still a baby. She couldn't . . . you don't mean, she is that clever?"

"She wants a pony."

Humphrey said, "We don't need to wait for her father to get well to say she may not have it. This we could not accept. It is time *we* were doing something for the Corees, in truth it is. I will call Mistress Dare. You will see."

Eleanor had been crying, Humphrey was sure, when she came out but her face glowed when she spoke. "Oh, Humphrey! Nias knew me just now. Roger Prat said it would happen any time. I . . . I cried, because I'm so happy. Women do."

Humphrey grinned at Manteo before he asked, "Did he ask for food?"

Lady of Roanoke

Eleanor laughed and made a wide circle with her arms. "Plates of it," she said, "he named things we haven't had since we left England. Roger says only broth still."

Manteo said, ponderously, "The White Doe is not to be anxious. My family will be happy to know that our friend talks again. We will set many snares, to make the broths."

"My husband will want to see Mary, to thank her," said Eleanor. "Bid her come, Manteo, when he is better?" Then she turned to Humphrey and eyed the puppy dubiously. "We haven't dirt floors here," she reminded him.

Humphrey smoothed the puppy's head and took his courage from deep inside. "There is another matter, Eleanor. This fellow is for Georgie and he can stay with Lion, an he tolerates him, coming from his own people. It's . . . there was to be a lamb for Virginia in the spring, Nias knew about it before he . . . he was willing then, with time to prepare a place. Now there is one, come out of season, but Virginia doesn't want it. Our little Lady of Roanoke has set her mind on one of Mary's ponies. I'm afraid she asked for it, Eleanor. A *pony* for Virginia, when some of the children haven't any kind of pet?"

Eleanor frowned, then she laughed. "Is *that* why her foot has hurt so much? The little minx. What shall we do when she's six or eight? Humphrey, please, I can't decide a thing like this and I don't know what Nias would say. She's the only girl her age but that excuse can go a little far. You'll have to do what seems best. I must go back to Nias. He will fret an I am not by." She smiled at them, worriedly, and shut the door.

Manteo said, "Now I must see to the snares. We will talk more. There is much to understand." And he was off.

Humphrey sat down on the big flat stone which provided a step up to the back door of the house and had himself a good worry. He felt a little forlorn that Eleanor had not thought he might like to step in and just look at Nias. He wouldn't have said a word. But she was excited. That was natural.

And he hadn't been able to speak to Manteo about his own problem, materials for the school. Foolish, he now saw, to have thought for help there. It was habit, to rely on Manteo. Worse than that, he had forgot to speak in the Patentees' meeting about inviting the younger Indian children to learn from the colony's teachers. Their elders might appreciate the offer if they did not.

He grinned at the thought and then he gloomed again. There were too many things to think about. How he had missed Nias in these long days of his illness, not to be able to talk over worries.

And now the little Lady of Roanoke was making everything harder. Who would look after a pony for her, even if he allowed her to accept one? There'd be a stable to build, too, and one knew what Mark Bennet would say to that.

He *could* tell Mary that they'd like a pony very

much indeed but not as a gift to Virginia alone. If all
the children had an interest, they must take turns feeding it—a much fairer thing, altogether—though it would
surely bring trouble with Virginia before she'd see it
that way. She had come just short of a spanking several
times during her father's illness.

Now, mayhap, the two big boys would help with
the stable. They weren't liking school, he could tell.
And as soon as the campfire was no longer a roaring
necessity at night, they'd be spoiling for something else
to do since they would no longer need to carry wood
for the fires. Somebody would have to carry water to
the women in the houses, regularly, until they could
find a well. Were the Patentees waiting for Nias to get
back to their deliberations before they decided to call
in the Indians and be shown how to dig for water?
Couldn't they do anything without him, unless a colonist prodded them?

A glance at the sun showed that school must be
over. So he stirred off his stone and went to find the
big boys. The men were gathering for the hot meal that
one of their number now cooked every day. It was
Henry Payne's turn and he directed Humphrey, point-
ing with his wooden ladle.

"John and Billy? Over there, in the shade of the
new houses, with Sampson and Martyn."

As Humphrey approached the four he heard a
sentence which made him decide to put off his request
and instead ask if he could eat with them today, because
Nias had come to his senses and Mistress Dare was busy

with him. 'Twould be a kindness to her, an they would welcome him. They would, so he left the puppy with the boys and went to Henry to get a bowl of food.

John and Billy were deep into their harangue of father and uncle, between mouthfuls, by the time Humphrey returned and sat down.

Part of what they were saying was reasonable and he listened with a growing wonder that the colony had come thus far without more trouble than they'd had, when so little thought seemed to have been given to a number of vital things.

CHARCOAL AND BIRCHBARK

13

John and Billy welcomed Humphrey with wild gestures, emphasizing their great wrongs.

"Why must we be put to lessons with babies?" Billy demanded vehemently. "You are the only one of the three of us, who likes to study. You and your Latin. Goin' to be a rector some day, eh? All it's good for."

Humphrey grinned. "There's something you don't know. I did Latin on Roanoke to keep from having to go back to England. 'Twas a bargain with Governor White, so he wouldn't make me return. An he should see my uncle in Yorkshire, he could say there was no harm to my learning done here. Now I want to go on with it because I like it."

"Faugh!" said Billy. "When it's learned, what do
you have? I've asked you that before, or John did, eh?
We want to work. Make things with our hands. There's
a mort we could do instead of sitting on a stone and
listening to rector, mornings. Oh, the singing is fine.
That Tom knows some rare good tunes. But *they* . . ."
he threw a hand in a gesture of disgust, toward his
uncle and John's father, "they listen and don't do a
thing for us."

"No, they don't," said young John. "What good
to me is it that my father is a Patentee? Tell me that."

John Sampson, man of so few words, set his empty
bowl on the grass, folded his hands and looked at
George Martyn and the three boys, studying each face
before he said, "If the children of the Patentees are not
in the school, how to make the rest of the colony send
theirs? Schoolin' is good for some, so all should sit."

Young John shook his head sadly, for his parent's
stubborn convictions. "You see, Humphrey?"

George Martyn said, "It's true argument. Can't
deny."

"What is better than school, in your minds? Tell
me, both of you," said Humphrey. "I can't talk to Nias
yet awhile, but Master Prat is a good reasoner. He has
helped me with my worries before now. I'll see . . ."

Billy said, "*You* got worries, Humphrey? With
nobody to boss you? Nobody to tend? 'Ceptin', of
course, when you want to. You study only Latin. You
get a choice and we don't. *Worries?*"

Humphrey felt laughter surging up from his stomach, as always, and didn't bother to remind Billy that

he had had charge of the planting, enough to worry anyone, still looked after Georgie and Virginia, seemed to take on himself with no effort an anxiety for the whole colony which the rector felt was wrong. It just happened. Now, why should he bother with these two boys whose father and uncle stubbornly wouldn't?

"Everyone has worries, Billy. You seem to have some. Tell me what you'd like to do," Humphrey urged again. "Mayhap I could get you a choice, too. I came to see you today because I've a special favor to ask . . . so . . .?"

"An you make things with your hands, you've got summat to show, at the finish. D'you know what Mark Bennet's got started? He's dryin' up some fine hardwood in a kind of earth oven he's made, to fashion trenails . . ." Billy's voice quivered with his interest.

"And what are those? New to me," said Humphrey.

"Those peg things you pound in holes to fasten two pieces of wood together, so dry that when you soak them, they get bigger and fill the hole forever and aye. Strong. Those are against the time he'll be making chairs and tables. I want to be put to that, Humphrey . . . it's worth doin'."

"The boy is right," said George Martyn. "But I wouldn't go against Sampson's idea of what's best for the whole colony, to get him his wish."

Humphrey said, to John's father, "But sir, haven't you thought of taking this up with all the Patentees? You and Nias and Roger Prat are the only fathers. The others haven't thought . . ."

CHARCOAL AND BIRCHBARK

Stubborn still, John Sampson shook his head. "'Twouldn't be right," he said, "to use my position so."

It was no use to argue at the moment, Humphrey saw. So he turned to the younger John.

"D'you want to make furniture, too?" he asked.

"You won't make a joke of my wish?" the boy asked, cautiously. "Billy did, first off."

"No more than he does of my Latin," Humphrey promised, grinning. "What's it?"

"I want a deerskin suit like yours and my father won't let me ask Manteo to have one made for me. He said I could have it an I'd shoot my own animals, cure the skins myself and sew it. I could do it, but we've got to do our share of the work, to earn our food—that's fair—so how're we going to learn making things if we have to go to school the same as little children?" He snapped his fingers.

"This company will always need clothes," said Humphrey, "and some doublets are much worn. Master Sampson, sir, I cannot see why you deny this boy. Give me leave to talk it out with someone? And you, Master Martyn?"

The two men looked at each other and finally nodded.

Young John said, "An Mary would teach me, I could learn how to dress skins almost right away. I've been watching how she does it. D'you know what she uses to soften a deer hide? Its brains." John made a face and said, "Ugh!"

Lady of Roanoke

Billy said, "I'd rather wear my old doublet and make a chair."

John ignored him. "The brain stuff is soft and takes the stiffness right out. And if there isn't enough of that, she takes green corn and squeezes out the pulp to rub on. There's something in the one or the other that makes a fair job."

Humphrey smoothed the knees of his deerskin trousers with new appreciation. While he had been doing Latin the boys had used their eyes. He himself had seen Manteo's people make a boat by burning out a log, but he had never seen a deerskin cured and prepared for sewing. The Indians knew how to do so many things. Whatever one learned from them, it was schooling of a sort.

There! Why not use that for a theme when he talked to Roger Prat? The Patentees could give it out to the whole colony that the headmaster was adding some special classes. Get the boys to come to catechism every morning and then spin off to woods and village. It was as good as done, he felt. John would be awkward at his tailoring, mayhap, unless he had a bent that way.

Aloud he said, "Now then, my special worry."

"You mean we can help *you*?" Billy asked, all his truculence forgot. "What's to do?"

"Build a pony stable."

"You startin' your farm already, Humphrey?"

"With one pony, my cow and Master Tusser's book of directions about husbandry? Nay, 'tis our little Lady of Roanoke has us in the toils again. Mary wants to give her a pony, though I think she was . . . well, somewhat persuaded to offer it."

The boys laughed and John said, "That baby girl has waited a mighty long time for someone to connect up her sore foot with one of Mary's Barbarys."

"And I, her godfather," said Humphrey, "was the first to be taken in. Now I have the deciding that we accept it or not and I think it should be for all the children. Virginia won't like that, but fair's fair, if we can keep to our position. They'll all have to help with the stabling and the feeding." He shook his head, ruefully. "Something else to see to and someone to settle their disputes. Who will that be? You two want the office?"

Father and uncle had drifted off to work, so there was no one to question the boys' decision. They looked at each other, and after a moment, both nodded.

Billy said, "It won't be the same as sittin' *with'm* in the school. They'll do as we say about the pony. So, we build it a stable, first?"

Humphrey nodded. "Can't bother Mark Bennet with it, and I wouldn't know how to begin."

John said, "Mark's all right. Not so growly lately. Sort of quiet. But we needn't ask him for a thing. We can do it. Sapling poles'd be best, eh, Billy? Set together nice and tight, double thickness, with mat roof maybe, and a place for Lion alongside, for protection like, and company. You come with us to get our fire wood, Humphrey, and we'll show you the kind. Take a few days to cut and trim enough. Any reason to hurry?"

Lady of Roanoke

It was on that first search for poles to make the stable wall that Humphrey found the answer to his worry about writing materials for the *Absey* class, and Thomas Warner's young mathematicians.

"Look, Humphrey, ain't this a pretty trick?" Billy was working away at the trunk of a tree which looked like a ghost in the deep shade of the woods, and it stirred a memory of Roanoke. "Mark Bennet showed us this. You can peel it any time of year. A handful makes a prize for starting a hearth fire. Look! Birchbark!" The lad held up a wide band, evenly cut right round the tree, several layers thick. "Indians use big pieces of it for canoes. Takes a mort of patience, getting it off the tree. Separate it down to thin, dry it a little and it's like paper. Could write on it, had you the means. What's the matter, Humphrey? You look struck."

"I am," he said, blinking as at a strong light. "I know birchbark. I just hadn't thought of it for the school. We could use it for the children to copy their letters on. The only thing I can think of for writing is goose quill nibs and those wouldn't be easy . . ."

"No, Humphrey, they wouldn't," said John. "Mark Bennet uses something to number the logs. So they fit in the right place after they're notched. It's black."

"He makes it," said Billy. "He got the trick at his old shipyard in Cornwall. The stories that man can tell . . ."

"You don't mean charcoal?" Humphrey asked, incredulously.

"Yes, that's it," said Billy, "and very dirtying on

the hands. Think of Little Amby's shirts. And what Mistress Viccars will say."

"Let her say," said Humphrey. "It's that much better than nothing. The children have to learn their letters." Then, more slowly, "But Master Bennet takes a great deal amiss. I don't see how I'm to approach him."

"We'll go with you, Humphrey. I told you he ain't so growly since some days past. What's come over him, nobody knows. You'll see."

Humphrey shouldered a load of brush and dead tree branches broken into carrying length and marched along with the two boys, wondering how his request would be received. The houses were going up rapidly. Mark was at the farther end of the green that afternoon where they were working on one of the bunkhouses for the single men.

How would Mark bear himself? Humphrey felt self-conscious as they approached and wished he hadn't heard the story of the man's rebuke at the hands of Thomas Warner, though he knew it had been told him to give the carpenter every chance to redeem himself. This would be the first time they had come face to face since that happening. He'd meet him halfway, or more.

He came toward them, didn't wait for their approach, which alone was surprising. He wasn't scowling, better still. He listened patiently to the excited boys, ventured to wink at Humphrey over their heads.

Lady of Roanoke

"It's only if you can spare some charcoal out of your present supply, Master Bennet," Humphrey qualified. "I wouldn't want you to stop the work, to burn more. But I thought . . . that is, it's to make the school more interesting . . . the children have nothing in their hands . . ."

Mark said frankly, "I'm glad you asked me, Humphrey. It gives me a chance to . . ." he hesitated and looked at the boys, and astonished them by not seeming to mind that they heard him say, "offer amends for my . . . Thomas Warner said I'd been showing bad grace. I urged for the school so I ought to help with the . . . the trimmings, like."

"A good word for it, Mark," said Humphrey. "But I . . . this has happened so fast . . . only today . . . that Master Warner doesn't know of it yet. Maybe you'd like to . . . would you suggest the birchbark and charcoal idea to him? It'd be natural, you talking for having the school, which he'd know about."

Mark rubbed his chin and looked down at his feet, first, then he straightened, met Humphrey's eye, touched his shoulder lightly and said, "Yes, boy, I'll do that. Thank you for the chance."

"So it was Master Warner who gave him the setdown," John remarked as the boys turned away with Humphrey to go and plan the stable. "There has been no little wonder."

"You needn't satisfy it," said Humphrey, firmly. "If Master Bennet wants to tell it, that's his business, and only his. Mind!"

CHARCOAL AND BIRCHBARK

"Wild horses," said John.

"Sticks and stones," said Billy.

Roger Prat listened gravely and nodded now and then, when Humphrey set forth the advantages of special classes in wood and leather work at their school, and said he would speak to Thomas Warner.

It finally took the spanking Virginia had been spoiling for, for weeks, to convince her that the promised pony would be shared and that though she was the only girl, she was only one of the nine children in the colony, Humphrey counting himself with the grown-ups for the moment. The pony just couldn't be hers alone.

When the chastisement was over the little culprit threw herself into Humphrey's arms and sobbed, accusingly, "But Mary said she'd give it to me."

Humphrey wondered how much good the spanking had done, after all. He sat her up on his knee and raised the little firm chin with his forefinger, so that she had to meet his eyes. He said, "Little Lady of Roanoke, tell me just one thing. Did you ask Mary to give you the pony?"

"She gives us lots of things."

"Did you ask for the pony?"

"I told her my foot hurt." Sniffle, sniffle.

"You've said that to a good many people here."

"But Mary is the only one who has little horses."

The stable was finished and the pony had arrived

before the arrangements were all made with Mary and Mark for the special classes for John and Billy. It involved a Patentees' meeting and a private session with the rector because school catechism time conflicted with the new plans. No announcements were made and the children had been so excited by the arrival of the pony and several near-fights over a name for it, that they hadn't been sensitive to the atmosphere around John and Billy, until the first morning they failed to appear.

That night, at bedtime, Humphrey was aware of unusual stirrings in the next pallet and when he was convinced of the reason he sat up and said, "Georgie, have you got the puppy in your bed?"

"Yes, Humphrey."

"He can't stay. You know that. You heard Eleanor and Mistress Betsey. What if he cries in the night and disturbs Nias? Come on, up! He'll have to go outside with Lion."

"Oh, Humphrey!"

"I'll go with you."

Lion accepted the puppy once more with a welcoming lick and they snuggled together into the leafy bedding of their stable-kennel.

Back in the house, Humphrey said, "Georgie, you had that dog in here because you had some kind of bad feeling. Any more fights? Tell me."

"Not bad ones. Just almost-ones. I don't like the name Robbie Ellis wants for the pony."

Humphrey yawned. "That's understandable. Is that all?"

"We-ll . . ."

"Georgie, I'm sleepy. Please!"

"I don't like school, Humphrey. I hate Latin. I want to learn about cows. I *like* cows. Little Amby's father will teach me all he knows about them."

"I doubt it. Not for a while, anyway. I suppose it's because John and Billy . . . oh, Georgie," Humphrey groaned, "they're *big* boys. When you're thirteen, Nias may consider it. That gives you five years to decide for sure. If my little cow said Moo to you, you'd run. Go to sleep!"

Of arms and a hero I sing, who first from the walls of Troy . . . Heroes left home to do their great deeds, Humphrey thought drowsily, but he had nowhere to go, except across the valley and into those blue, misty distances. What lay beyond them?

NEW YEAR REFLECTIONS

14

It was John Brooke's custom—had been, in England, before he became a Raleigh colonist—to write in his diary on New Year's Eve a summary of the happenings important to him, of the previous twelve-month.

He was a man of some foresight, as well, an odd mixture of business acumen and near-saint in his chosen consecration to the service of his church. His thought had been to spend a few years with the colony, start them nicely in the establishing of their Christian roots and practices, and then return to England. But his preparation for those years, which later covered a life time, had been practical, too, to the point of having a

NEW YEAR REFLECTIONS

printer bind up a pile of blank folios for his diaries. He would need them, he thought, to preserve the wonders of the New World which he had been told were fantastic, beyond all reckoning.

Fragments of the pages for the year 1590, pieced together painfully by his children when their need of such comfort was great—and later lost by succeeding generations until the carefully penned lines lived only in memory—recorded John Brooke's awe, on that first New Year's Eve in their new home, that he should be so singularly blessed as to have fallen in love with a good woman. It had dawned upon him, only that day, and he was still dazed by it.

Until that moment, like many another before him, he had thought the Church enough. He had his pipe and good colony food for physical comfort and the services on Sundays with such sacraments as fell between—All Saints Day and the like, only one baptism so far, little Anne Viccars—for his soul's sake. Latterly was added his Latin teaching. All sufficing. No, not quite. Virginia Dare, the little featherhead, he mused, was sadly wanting in appreciation of that ancient speech and would sooner run at Humphrey Hall's heels than study anything. Surely a child of three years and a bit could learn *amo, amas, amat,* an she tried. She expressed the meaning clearly enough every moment she was with Humphrey and he looked upon her as a little sister. He *was* fourteen years older.

John Brooke smiled as he wrote and then he was stabbed with a grievous wound, though only in his mind.

Lady of Roanoke

How, please God, was he to marry, when he was the only clergyman, as far as he knew, in the whole New World? He groaned and let his pen rest.

Margery Harvie's geese provided him quills in plenty and he had only to trim them for use. He sat idly dividing and smoothing the barbs of the present one while he thought on his dilemma.

How fortunate that no one knew or suspected, except mayhap the dear object of his devotion, that he had any thought of marrying, and he wasn't sure about her. He thought back to recent weeks and before them, reviewing his conduct during the many calls he had made upon Ananias during his long illness and slow recovery. With the school in the Governor's room before the Long House was built, it had been so easy to step through into the family room and natural that he should see Mistress Glane at least once every day, if not oftener. Her invitations to the many meals he had partaken at the Dares' board had always seemed so naturally given—his presence a pleasure for Nias, recovering, and an accommodating expedient on the evenings he sat with Humphrey for his Latin lesson.

Had he done or said anything that would betray a special regard he hadn't known he felt? It was impossible not to notice how very comely Eleanor's helper was, how gracefully she fitted into the household, how beautiful she looked when tending young William. Why hadn't he recognized his feelings earlier? Now, the exact moment when he had fallen in love didn't matter a whit.

NEW YEAR REFLECTIONS

The Indians were not believers and had their own mysterious ceremonies of marriage, which he had never probed. Should he now speak to Manteo and . . . Oh, no, no that was not the way, only an expedient. What would the Indians think, particularly Manteo, who had been baptized on Roanoke and came to Sunday worship faithfully?

In England there would have been his Vicar in his own parish church to say the holy words or his Bishop, or a fellow priest in London. Yet how, being there, might he have had the opportunity to meet Mistress Betsey, she from Stafford and he of Devon? It had to be here in the greenwood with no priest to bless them.

It was then, at some moment in that midnight hour of questioning and despair, that from somewhere, out of his musings or communings, that he had the thought— *you could ordain one.*

Could he? It sent him searching the prayer book for the exact wording of the ritual of ordination:

It is evident unto all men, diligently reading Holy Scriptures and ancient Authors, that from the Apostles' time there have been these Orders of Ministers in Christ's Church, Bishops, Priests and Deacons. Which offices were ever more had in such reverend estimation, that no man might presume to execute any of them, except he were first called, tried, examined, and known to have such qualities as are requisite for the same; and also by public Prayer, with Imposition of Hands, were approved and admitted thereunto by lawful Authority.

Lady of Roanoke

The only lawful body they had was the Patentees, though the most thoughtful must have long since realized they were no longer a colony, subject to the Queen. How could they be when there was no communication? But the matter now in hand was, would all the people accept the *lawful authority* of the Patentees, in lieu of a church body, to choose a colonist possessed of the qualities *requisite for the same*, to be a priest? With the power to celebrate the marriage sacrament? Would they?

Who, what man among them could qualify? Who would be willing to undergo the study and preparation that would make him a candidate for ordination, an he, John Brooke, could persuade Nias Dare to lay it before his fellows?

Further, must the underlying reason be boldly given? He hadn't yet approached Mistress Betsey, but might be able to, before the meeting, if someone in the colony would prepare the way for him. She had no family, saving the Dares. Mayhap Mistress Dare would act? That would be the decisive thing, he now saw, for if Mistress Betsey had a fixed mind for some other colonist, then there'd be no need of the meeting. Not precipitately, though of a truth, there should be a second clergyman for the colony in any case. That had not occurred to him until this midnight revelation.

But, assuming Mistress Betsey's mind to run with his, there was another question, equally portentous. The Patentees must be satisfied of their right to sit and weigh a churchly matter. He searched the prayer book again.

NEW YEAR REFLECTIONS

But all he could find was an indication of some lenience in the preface, which might serve:

In worship different forms and usages may without offence be allowed provided the substance of the Faith be kept entire; and that what cannot be clearly determined must be referred to Discipline, and by common consent and authority, may be amended, or otherwise disposed of, as may seem most convenient for the edification of the people, according to the various exigency of times and occasions.

The harassed man read it several times and thought, finally, that that should satisfy anyone. A sacrament of marriage was worship, surely.

He had another consoling thought. He'd not have to seek a Bishop and two Justices of the Peace for a license, as required at home. There was no Bishop of Virginia and so far the colony had not appointed even one Justice of the Peace. The Patentees still administered everything and so they truly were the *Discipline* to be referred to, in the language of the prayer book.

When he finished his writing and rose from the desk to seek his bed he murmured *and a happy issue out of all their difficulties.*

Ananias Dare, no diarist, took mental stock of the year, next morning, New Year's Day, sitting in front of his house after breakfast, to view the fair prospect before him.

All of the dwellings were now built, safe and snug on their stone floors and smoke was rising from every chimney. The outdoor cooking place was roofed over as a shelter for Henry Berry's anvil. Behind it a long shed provided storage room and work shops.

The sound of Henry's hammer and the iron ringing was pleasant, though Ananias wondered, among other daily worries, how long the metal things they had brought, would last. Even Henry's skill couldn't make them do forever.

The Long House, erected last, had been changed somewhat from the first plan. One end, closed off with a proper thick log partition, was now their chapel and it had its own fireplace. Also, it had stout, casemented windows on the side opposite the door to let in light when there was need.

There were no pews in it, only some stools which Billy Wythers had made for practice work. That would be remedied in time, as fast as Mark's men could turn out necessary furniture for all the dwellings.

The colony was fortunate, altogether. They were not experiencing the kind of cold here that they had known severally in Yorkshire and Devon and the Midlands of England. This was a mild country, compared. And Humphrey had done well with his harvest. The bountiful yield was greater far than crops any husbandman among them had ever garnered at home.

Ananias had two particular worries out of many that he could have chosen to dwell on that morning. One was the babblings in his illness when his mind wandered. When he begged to be told what he had said, everyone assured him it was just nonsense. Try as he would he could not detect any change in the attitude of the colonists toward the authority of the Patentees, no questioning of their decisions. Indeed, if by any miracle John White or a deputy should penetrate this far inland, he would find in all semblance a flourishing colony of the Queen.

His other anxiety was for two of the colonists. Did John Brooke or Betsey Glane have such colossal self-deception that they thought no one guessed their deep feelings, one for the other? Had it occurred to the rector that there was no one to marry them? They had been right circumspect but the situation was fretting Eleanor and she daily urged him to resolve it, refusing to see that it was not his duty.

Merely thinking on it made him restless, so he wrapped the folds of his great cape a little closer about his spare frame to walk out from the fringe of trees which protected his house for a look at the hills.

Mark and his men had built a seat where the park land sloped to the stream and he had so arranged the houses in the open, within Thomas Warner's measurements, that most had a clear view across the valley. The changing colors on the hills as the year advanced to autumn and on to winter had delighted everyone. The Looking Seat was a long, split log, rubbed smooth on its flat surface and anchored at each end and in the middle to stones half sunk in the turf and hollowed out to receive the round side snugly.

Someone else had come forth this fine morning, Ananias saw, but he was pacing, eyes on his feet and indifferent to the soft blue of the hills. With autumn's colors gone, the evergreens had emerged from background to first place again, blending, as they had in summer, into the vaporous distance.

The pacer was the rector and he greeted Ananias with more than usual warmth and grip of hand. "Nias, I must talk to you," he blurted, "a grave matter, for the Patentees later, but for your ear alone first. I came out here to study how to lay it before you and now you are come and . . . Nias, I want to be married and . . ."

"And there is no one to conduct the sacrament for you," Ananias finished for him. "You've finally seen it."

"Only last night, man, did I know I wanted it, so how could you tell me my thought this morning?" The rector looked amazed.

"Because 'tis writ on your face, and on the lady's, too, the moment you meet—has been for many a day," Ananias explained. "What can you do? I've thought of it until my mind is weary. Unless, mayhap, there is one among us who has served his parish or his hundred at home as Justice of the Peace, whose duty might be stretched to compass the matter? Think you?"

"Not of that, no," said John Brooke, "but another way, an all agree to it. And better for the colony than your idea. Walk with me and ponder. Mind, Nias Dare, 'tis not entirely for my own wishes, but a practical matter that should have been weighed before now. Suppose I were taken from you, by accident or Nature's design, who then would minister unto the people?

NEW YEAR REFLECTIONS

There will be other baptisms, I hope, and marriages, and burials to come, as our lives go on unto their appointed end. Think well on this, Nias. The time has come to ordain another priest who will be in all things to this colony what my own endeavors have been, to guide as a shepherd."

The sun climbed higher as the two men paced and reached zenith before Ananias Dare was convinced enough of the arguments and the clear authority they had in the prayer book to do as John Brooke urged, to call a meeting of the Patentees.

" 'Tis a grave matter, this calling of a man who has not heretofore had any conviction within himself to take churchly orders, to thus suddenly be faced with such duty," said Ananias, finally. "Who of us is worthy, John Brooke? Not I, surely."

"The ballot will tell. The right man will be chosen. You'll see, Nias. Call me the meeting."

PATENTEES' MEETING

15

Eleanor's first thought, when Ananias told her that she need not now urge him further about the rector's romance, was practical.

"That means vestments," she said. "The new chaplain will need a whole set, and while 'tis true that John Brooke shan't be wearing his to be wed, haven't you noticed that he looks a little frayed around the edges? He should have all new, too, along with a wife to look after his shirts. What *can* we make them of?"

Ananias said, "Men don't fall in love for the sake of shirts. He thinks it happened last night, that he became aware of it only then, while writing in his diary."

Eleanor rolled her eyes in eloquent disbelief. They two were alone in the kitchen and she sat with her chin propped on her hands looking dreamily at nothing. So Ananias was startled when she exclaimed, "Petticoats!"

"Wh-a-a-t?"

"For surplices and shirts, Nias. We all wear several, as husbands know. They can be cut up and will make as good fine white vestments as we could order out from London, and enough pieces left over for some shirts."

He said, "Please, Eleanor, an the Patentees agree, the chosen one may be a married man. Let his wife donate her petticoats to his new state. And there is no hurry, whatsover. He will have to study with the rector until he is ready for the ordination."

Eleanor looked at him, wide-eyed and innocent and he realized that it was the way their little Lady of Roanoke looked when bent on scheming.

"Of course a married man, Nias," she agreed. "Who could they choose but you?"

"Nay, nay," he protested. "An the ballot comes that way, I shall refuse. I'm not worthy. Besides there is my health, not yet secure, which makes it not right that I be chosen, with perhaps the choice to be made all over again too soon, were I to . . . no matter. Above all other thoughts, I am still acting Governor and Chief Patentee. Let the responsibilities be shared."

Eleanor looked disappointed. "The vestments would become you so, Nias," she mourned. "Your tallness and the way your hair grows, but . . ." with a deep sigh, "as you say, it lies with the ballot. You are almost always right. Though not now about your health. I will not have it that you may not completely recover."

Whereupon she clapped her hands to her head in dismay. "What a careless one am I. Your potion, Nias. Why did you not remind me?"

He made a wry face. " 'Tis best forgot. The longer I put it off, the better. Let it be, for once. Where Mary finds the herbs she brews it from is beyond me. No greenwood could hold so many with such an appalling flavor."

"They're dried, in little bags, hung from the framework of her mat house, as I well know," said Eleanor, blandly. "You shall have it now."

She brought him the mixture, wild honey with the potent herbs, but bitter withal, and stood before him while he drank, in quick gulps and holding his breath, to avoid the taste.

"Ugh!" he remarked, when he handed her the empty cup, "The means is better than the potion. A right graceful bowl."

"Aye, Nias, but 'tis the brew that keeps you well."

"Then all the household, nay, the whole colony, should drink it with me," he growled.

Eleanor handled the cup carefully, with a housewifely satisfaction that the Dares now had good earthen dishes to set on their table, as the other colonists had, and more to come, from the hands of the earnest potters—Clement and Chapman and their helpers—who had learned a new skill by Mary's patience—plates and bowls and cups, albeit those had no handles. That was beyond Mary's talent.

Eleanor Dare was never to know that her father had already written in his reports to authorities that the earthen vessels in which the Indians cooked their stews *are so large and fine that our potters with large wheles can make noe better.*

Before he left for the Patentees' meeting that afternoon, Nias cautioned Eleanor about secrecy. "Usually you are discerning about what may be said and what not, outside our house, but today I must remind you that because 'tis romance that's toward and women love the circumstance, no word may pass about this deliberation. I cannot tell how they will deal with it. They do not know why they are coming together. As usual, I gave Humphrey no reason when I bade him summon them. Unless one or another has an inkling, they will not dream it's about a wedding."

"But Nias . . ."

"Nay, hear me out, wife. Rector has not yet offered to Mistress Glane and it would be embarrassing for her, if any word were spoken of it, too soon." When Eleanor's face puckered, he added, "She will need to prepare and it's altogether too early for the matter to be bandied about. You must see it as only reasonable."

"Nias Dare!" Eleanor was laughing, and he was relieved to find that the pucker was not the forerunner of tears. But what was she saying? He couldn't believe what he heard.

"*Nias!* Married to me all these years and you have no idea that the preparations are already toward? We've been busy with the dyepot these many days and you'd never guess where we got the dress our bride will walk in. A Joseph's coat, really, but now a most elegant dark red. 'Twill do her years for best."

He shook his head at her, solemnly, having no words to reply.

The Patentees gathered for that most portentous meeting with mixed feelings. It was a lovely bright afternoon and a game of bowls was planned. They had been nurturing a special green, smooth and beautiful where the great campfire had been, for that end. There was also the anticipated pleasure of the colony feast in the evening. It was as inconvenient an hour or day, therefore, as could be chosen, but if Nias Dare felt it important enough to precede bowls there must be a good reason. Humphrey had known nothing when any had tried to question him.

The meeting was held in the chapel, where a bright fire livened the air because the heavy wooden windows had to be opened for light. A large basket of pine cones and chips from Mark Bennet's carpenter shop stood by, ready to renew the flame when the log burned through.

Humphrey had made the fire and filled the basket and was much puzzled to be told by Nias to bring plenty of small pieces of birchbark and some charcoal sticks from the school supply, ready for balloting, should there be any. He was to sit outside the door on call, moreover, to distribute the ballots and later, to count them. He had had another idea about a good way to spend that afternoon, a shoot with fowling pieces borrowed from Roger Prat's storehouse and Manteo for companion, so Georgie was sent flying to the village to say he couldn't come.

Why were the Patentees meeting? Everything seemed to be going so well in the colony. The school established. No one ill, except Nias's continuing ails. And he had met the Indians' chief at last and found him a tired old man, completely under Mary's thumb. No quarrels lately, either, after the question about the geese had been talked out to the point of the Harvies and Warners changing houses, so that the birds were close to the Viccars' cow yard, thus bringing all offense together in one spot.

Humphrey chuckled. The colonists liked the goose eggs and the milk, but people had to grumble about something. Then he yawned and called for the children to come and relieve his boredom, when Georgie came back. It wouldn't hurt the little Lady of Roanoke to say her numbers for him. She had a singular distaste for learning, even the simple things Mistress Mannering imparted. And Georgie couldn't spell. He needed hints most days.

The Patentees drifted in, one by one, spoke to Humphrey and when all had arrived the door was closed. It was a thick one, swung on stout leather hinges. Unfortunately, for their curiosity, the windows though open were all on the side opposite the door, so that neither the children nor Humphrey could hear a word that went on.

He'd have liked seeing Ananias rise to open the meeting. The thinning caused by his illness had given him a distinguished air, aided by the gray hairs that had appeared above his ears.

Nias nodded to Dion Harvie, who solemnly called the roll: Dare, Bayly, Cooper, Sampson, Stevens, Prat, Harvie, Nichols, Dimmocke, White. Only one absent. It was a courtesy they never missed, reading that last name. There had been two others, once. George Howe, now deceased, and Simon Ferdinando, whose name was ignored. He had betrayed his trust by disobeying Sir Walter about their colony site, refusing to go into Chesapeake Bay.

No one was surprised to see the rector present. He was often invited to their sessions, as who had better right. He sat in the pulpit with Nias, as was the custom when he came.

After the roll call, Nias looked at John Brooke, who shuffled his feet and shook his head, so Nias rose and began, most awkwardly for him, to state the purpose of the meeting. Why had he seemed to want the rector to do it?

When he had finished, they sifted out of his many whereases and wherefores the idea that the colony should have a second chaplain, someone they could choose, oddly enough, by authority construed from the Prayer Book, because John Brooke might at any time be taken from them and where would they be left, for the ministrations to their souls, that any group like-situated in the whole world needed at some times more sorely than at others. He hadn't said why it seemed so important that they meet on a holiday for considering the use of that strange authority they didn't know they had. Until today.

When he asked John Brooke to speak to the matter, the rector stumbled to his feet, turned bright red and then went so astonishingly white that they began to look at each other in alarm. Was he already sickening for something for which there might be no remedy? Had Nias a too-imperative reason for calling them together?

"Your . . . our Chief Patentee . . . has s-s-spoken truly," the rector managed to gasp, "and he has touched upon an . . . an exigency . . . a real need . . . that I should have . . . ah . . . taken up with you . . . ah . . . much earlier. But it didn't occur to me . . . ah . . . until . . ." here he looked at Nias imploringly, and was told crisply to go on, be done with it, which made him pull himself together somewhat, "until recently, last night to be exact, when it is my custom . . . ah . . . has been for many years to . . . to . . . well, I review the old year."

The Patentees were bored and looked at each with raised eyebrows now and squirmed in their seats. Wanton waste of a good afternoon at bowls, and what did the man mean? He was now examining his fingernails, then looking at the floor, anywhere but at them, which did provide an opportunity to see that he was shaking all over and his face had again become so red that he seemed in danger of falling in a fit.

Indeed, Chris Cooper half rose in his place, thinking to prevent it happening.

But the poor man didn't fall. He found the edges of his cape and clutched them, as was his wont with his stole on Sundays when he preached. Indeed, he seemed to take heart from the act, for he went on then, straightly and firmly to say what must be said.

"I had thought to take this matter step by step, now that it has had to be brought to you, and had I thought of it, as far back as Roanoke, the reason would still have been wise and good. Now I have two reasons."

He glanced again at Nias, who smiled benignly, and the Patentees wondered the more. It couldn't be that rector sir was making such a to-do about his love for Betsey Glane? It had been plain to read this long time, so the womenfolk said.

"But I cannot stand before you longer this afternoon to argue for the first, an I did not also make known to you that I . . . gentlemen, I have found a truth which all must recognize, that in every priest there is a man like yourselves, with the same human emotions and I'd like to be . . . I am asking that one of you, or other colonist, qualify to marry me, preside at my marriage sacrament. But it would have been a mockery of holy orders, had we not, Nias and I, first weighed for you the general need that the colony should never be left desolate with no minister at all."

He sat down abruptly, and, too shy to look at them

immediately, buried his face in his hands for a moment so that only Nias saw the dawning understanding among the Patentees and their delight in the rector's news. It was clear they hadn't thought about the need for another rector. So, who could qualify?

Nias rose, smiling and said, quietly, "With our understanding sharpened by what we have just heard, is it your pleasure to act as it has been shown we have authority to do, and decide that this colony may have another chaplain to assist our rector? I think on that we may take a rising vote. Will those who agree, please stand?"

They rose as one man and when the rector raised his head, Nias turned to him with a little gesture, as much as to say, "There you are, sir!"

When they sat down, he went on, "Now that you have so voted, it is our duty to choose some member of this colony, to be that chaplain, the one man who, an he be willing, is best qualified in *character, person, speech, and known principles* to take such part of holy orders as is possible by the means we have, to minister unto you and me and all here in this settlement, in the manner we have always respected in John Brooke. If you have no questions I propose that we sit quietly for a time, to think on this matter and when you are ready to vote, each will signify by uplifted hand. I have Humphrey waiting outside with ballots. And in his own good time and the lady's, our rector will announce his plans."

John Brooke asked then to be excused and when

Lady of Roanoke

he had gone, quietly, with his head bowed as he did when leaving church after the benediction, there was no other sound except a sigh, here and there, a superficial cough, the crackling of the fire, and the usual outdoor noises—the honk of a Harvie goose, far across the green, a mother calling a child—it sounded like Elizabeth Viccars and Little Amby right outside the chapel door at Humphrey's feet that very minute.

Then one by one the hands went up and when there were eight Nias went to the door and Humphrey came in, to distribute his bits of birchbark. Nias took one, too, and Humphrey waited while the charcoal sticks were gripped hard to write a name. He collected them and Nias said he could stay right there to announce the count.

"Prat," he began, aloud, and "Prat," he read again and wondered what the poor feckless one, no, not feckless now, doing more than one man's work . . . "Prat," again and again to the count of eight and only one ballot read "Dare," so Roger hadn't voted for himself.

They laughed, when Humphrey looked at them, bewildered, and Dion Harvie said, "Tell the lad, Nias, he keeps his tongue when it is necessary."

Nias said, "Not until we are finished," and turned to Roger to ask the proper question. "You have heard the count, Roger Prat. How do you say?"

The chaplain-designate hesitated. "I had no thought to be chosen. There are better men here than I." He looked around and saw encouragement on every face. "Perhaps, after I have studied, there should be another vote, before the ordination. Meantime, I thank you, gentlemen. I will try to merit the honor."

They crowded round then to shake his hand and Nias said, "Now, Humphrey, it's like this."

BETSEY GLANE'S WEDDING

16

The colony received the news of the rector's engagement with its usual demeanor. Excitement, personal interest, gossip and curiosity blended equally in the fashion of ingredients for making a fine Christmas cake.

The circumstance of this colony romance was so different from the other two. Jane Berry had been a widow when she joined the other colonists at Plymouth. And Henry Berry hadn't let on he was so much as looking for a wife before their banns had come up for first reading in the tiny chapel on Roanoke.

Nor had Margaret Jones let anyone know she had left her heart on the ship until Tom-the-Lute had stayed behind and announced his intention to cast his fate with that of the colony.

Roger Prat's coming ordination took second place, dismissed by solemn wonder and sorry headshakes at what the colony might have come to, had rector, sir, not fallen in love. He could have died, as easily, taken by the same kind of fever Nias Dare had, and then what about christenings and burials? Or the marriage sacrament for the three spinsters that his passing would have left still unbespoke? Well, he *had* fallen in love instead of dying so that left only two women to be considered.

Jane Mannering, happy at teaching, and Emma Merrimoth, looking after the Harvie geese because Margery was hoping to have her baby before the wedding, were not present at the sewing gatherings. Nor was the bride-to-be. It wouldn't be proper.

It was embarrassing as well as awkward that Roger Prat hadn't a wife to provide the necessary petticoats for his vestments. What married woman wanted to give up a prized cambric garment for such a purpose?

And how were they to find out the state of Roger's shirts? Had he a spare one he could let go long enough for them to take a measure from it and then cut and sew? Could they get the right size for his cotta, from the shirt? Rector's would be too large for Roger.

When Nias was consulted he volunteered to borrow an old shirt from Roger.

Eleanor lamented the necessity. "You should have let the women vote on the candidate. We'd have been more practical. Though you get the shirt from Roger, there is nothing to make new ones from."

Nias said, "You'd vote by the line of a man's hair and the way he trims his beard and if he's said his marriage vows? Oh, come, woman!"

"Roger Prat's beard is the best one in the colony. I've said naught against it."

"Then fancy how well it will look above his vestments and draw lots among you as to who will donate a petticoat for the service of the Church."

"Lots? I favor that. Thank you, Nias. Maybe 'twill work."

It didn't need to come to that.

One evening, before Nias had acted on his promise to borrow for pattern, Humphrey came in late for his meal, with a large bundle under his arm and a wide grin on his face. The rector was a guest, which made what happened doubly embarrassing for the women.

Before Eleanor or Georgie, with their usual curiosity, could ask what he carried, he had whipped the bundle open and spread it out on the floor mats beside the table, for all to see. It was a great wheel of beautifully fine cambric, hand stitched, with many tucks and edged with lace—a woman's long, full petticoat.

Humphrey bowed to Eleanor above it. "A gift to the Church, ma'am, for Master Prat's vestments."

He stooped and gathered it up again, rolling it carefully along the waistband and was making for Eleanor's bedroom with it before she could speak. Her face was scarlet and so was Humphrey's because he wanted so much to laugh.

BETSEY GLANE'S WEDDING

"Humphrey Hall!"

"Ma'am?"

"Not one step more, and no supper, until you tell me . . ."

"An I go hungry for a week, Eleanor, I may not tell who, and you have seen what it is, as nice a piece of muslin as . . ."

"Humphrey!"

Nias thumped the table with an angry fist so that the dishes knocked together.

"I've told all I may. Please. I only meant a little fun." He turned toward the others and looked at Eleanor and Betsey in turn. "Truly, I meant no harm. An I could tell you, all would agree with the humor of it. But that is what I promised not to do . . . almost on my life. Who shall say what the reason may be for such secrecy? Perhaps the giver couldn't write and yet wanted the gift fully explained?"

"All our women can write," said Eleanor, indignantly. She looked at Nias. "Let be. Put it away, Humphrey, and come and eat before the food is cold. Betsey has made us an excellent roast. The Sampson boy shot a deer and divided it among several of the families. I should ask him and his father for a meal . . ."

Humphrey put the skirt away and came to his place beside Georgie, who looked up at him with a scared expression.

Virginia, on the other side, said, "You're going to get a spanking, Humphrey."

The laughter helped the awkward moment and the general talk, interrupted by the petticoat, was resumed.

Lady of Roanoke

Apparently it was about a dwelling for the engaged couple, how large it ought to be and where the site.

Humphrey let the details slide over his head while he ate. He knew that somehow Mark Bennet should be warned to build two houses while he was about it. But was this his responsibility? If one word about a close personal thing was shared with one other colonist, every member of the colony eventually knew it.

He looked at Nias, thoughtfully, at the thin, fine face and the eyes expressing the good mind, a thoroughly trustworthy person. Tell him, as Chief Patentee, and he'd know what to do. Nias didn't often express his impatience with anyone as vehemently as he had just now. How nearly they had lost him. The colony wouldn't be the same place without Nias.

The venison was perfect. They hadn't asked him, but he, Humphrey, could tell them where the rector and Betsey should live. Right here with a room added on, that's where. Mayhap it would come that way in the end. Rector was a generous body and he might be willing to trade with . . . oh, oh, Humphrey, don't even think the names.

The wedding date was set the third week in April, so as to come after Lent. The women were all pleased. It gave them time to do all they thought they must, seeing that the ordination would be first.

The cold weather, though not as cold as on Roanoke, the restlessness of housed children, the spinning and weaving with all other daily duties, even the birth of Margery Harvie's little son, gave place to the ordination and wedding preparations.

Sometimes the work extended into the night because they now had lighting—the bayberry candles which Emma Merrimoth, quiet gentlewoman, had learned how to make from the Indians. She toiled endlessly at them, besides looking after the Harvie geese.

When Mark Bennet heard of her added work he set Billy Wythers to making sticks for the candles. They were fashioned from fat pine cones, hollowed out just enough to hold a taper firmly. The wider-opened petals at the base caught the drip and provided finger hold to carry them by.

The ordination service was held the week before the wedding. The petticoat gift had been put through such excellent cutting and needlework that no one would know, unless they did know, that it was the source of the spotless cotta Roger Prat was finally qualified to wear.

As Chief Patentee, Nias presented the candidate. He read from the ritual:

Good People, This is he whom we purpose God willing, to receive this day unto holy Office of Priesthood, for after due examination we find him lawfully called and meet for the same . . .

Then John Brooke offered the consecration prayer, *that he may duly execute his office to the edifying of Thy Church,* and all the people responded, *We beseech Thee to hear us, Good Lord.*

Afterward, just before the service ended, a profound silence fell, broken only by the muted call of mourning doves, deep in the forest. The matter had been accomplished, and Roger Prat could now serve as their chaplain, together with John Brooke. In the minds of some of the colonists that wildwood service made England and old ties there seem farther away than it yet had.

The wedding was not as solemn. There was music, for one thing, and much bright color that had not been a part of the ordination. The rich red of the bride's dress. The concomitant finery of the other women, long folded away in their chests. The masses of flowering fruit branches, gathered by Humphrey and John and Billy that morning. And Georgie Howe and Virginia, hand in hand, in blue velvet suit and hat and long dress and bonnet, to lead the bride to the chapel and along the short aisle to the altar.

The Wedding Hymn was a surprise for everyone. No one had paid much attention to the children lately, except to be glad they were in school. Tom-the-Lute had taken his class deep into the greenwood for practice and had so impressed the little ones that this was to be their gift to the rector and Betsey, and, as such, must not be told, that the secret was well kept. At least, if it was talked of, it had been listened to only vaguely.

John and Billy condescended to appear with the little group when they gathered promptly in the aisle

from their places in the congregation, after Roger Prat
had finished the ceremony and the kneeling couple
rose, to face their friends. Tom played softly for the
children to sing and directed with his chin.

Lovely kind, and kindly loving,
Such a mind were worth the moving;
Truly fair, and fairly true,
Where are all these but in you?

Wisely kind, and kindly wise—
Blessed life, where such love lies!
Wise, and kind, and fair, and true,
Lovely live all these in you.

Sweetly dear, and dearly sweet—
Blessed, where these blessings meet!
Sweet, fair, wise, kind, blessed, true,
Blessed be all these in you!

A MEDLEY OF YEARS

17

*(Being Excerpts from the
Private Diaries of John Brooke,
Written between the Years 1591 and 1600)*

New Year's Eve, *1591*

Another twelve-month vanished, going faster than any other I can recall in the whole of my life before, particularly the time since our wedding. The hastening has not been because we were settling into our own house, though one was built. We are under the Dares' roof and likely to be, for some time. Mark Bennet added two rooms on the side toward the hills. Now I may have my own study with an outside door to it, to receive troubled colonists, which is more than I had when a bachelor. Mark himself was one of my first serious visitors. He has never been confirmed. It may yet happen, an he takes the counsel I gave him.

The Rectory is occupied by our latest bride and groom, the which romance somewhat startled the colony, mayhap because its secret was kept very well, though afterward several people were sure they had seen the signs before others did. We are so fond of hindsight.

Humphrey Hall, our young orphan lad who is so responsible beyond his years, was the first person to be told, because Jane Mannering entrusted her best cambric petticoat to him, to help the women out when they needed material for Roger Prat's vestments. With it she had to confide her secret, their secret, though the man gave me no sign on the occasion of our wedding that I'd be called upon to do the same for him in a few months' time.

When Manteo and his people came back from their summer fishing on the Sound they brought two more Barbary ponies. Mary is building up a respectable stable. They run wild and have to be tamed so it is now clearer why Humphrey was so shocked that Virginia asked Mary for one. Now I know, too, that the Corees have made well-marked trails from here to their people south and westward, and they go back and forth with pack-loads. They are a sturdy race. They also brought news of John White. He came back, seeking us, but was prevented from making prolonged search by the ship's people, with whom he seemed in disfavor. The poor unfortunate man! Though a few realized that coming here would cut us off from England for the rest of our lives, the knowledge that the Governor did try to find us was somehow comforting. It caused some soul-searching and confession and public acknowledgment that a good many of the colonists have had the same thought as mine from the beginning, but felt if it was ignored and we kept on with the leadership of the Patentees, we'd have more order. The idea has been proved wise and we are used to the greenwood now.

New Year's Eve, 1592

This has been a heartbreaking year for Betsey and me. Our first born, Cedric Hatton Brooke, was a puny babe and lingered with us a bare six weeks. It is well one has no means of seeing into the future. Would I have been fainthearted and forsworn my contract to come to the New World an I could have known that my son would be the first to lie in our colony's burial ground? The loss has taken the heart out of my lovely girl and she is only now rising to laughter again.

At Whitsun I christened Megan Jones' baby brother, Arthur, and another son for the Berrys—James, the how-manyeth, I do not know, in that large family.

Last week Henry Rufotte, oldest of the colonists, joined our babe on the cleared knoll that faces the blue hills. He was taken by the same fever that Nias had, though nursed as faithfully by the Prats together.

Their young Johnnie is showing a real aptness for Thomas Warner's figures.

New Year's Eve, 1593

This year the Indian children began sitting with ours in the school. We owe the tribe a great gift, with little at hand to acknowledge it, except our learning, when they have literally preserved our lives, though I often wonder to what purpose. I foresee some intermarriage among the generation that will grow up together the more closely now, but what matter? We are in the greenwood to stay. There is one little lad called Oppy who favors Virginia, much to Georgie Howe's disgust. It has caused a few fights, which distress Humphrey.

Mistress Prat organized a May fete for the children. Only the shadow of what some of us knew in England, no morris figures possible, or other revel. But Tom Jones brought out the proper music for winding the May Pole and it was something vastly different for our humdrum life. I am minded to use one of my diary folios to write out all Tom's songs. He has a way of putting heart in us when we most need it, though he seems a lazy fellow and his family would suffer, an we did not hold all staples in common.

New Year's Eve, 1594

Humphrey Hall was twenty-one last April and Nias finally let him move to his own house, which Mark Bennet built in a great clearing in the woods back of the plow lands that lie between us and the Indian village. He took Georgie with him, twelve now, a weed's growth they have at that age. This place seemed strangely quiet when they had gone. The little Lady of Roanoke was not to be comforted. She takes it hard that life brings changes not always of one's choice, liking it better on her terms. I sometimes resist my Betsey's lesser whims, just from living in the same house with that child! Humphrey is a born farmer and he continues to be head of the planting, though he has never received the outright gift of land that he hoped for when we came. Yet the tribe has never taken back the fields they assigned to us in the beginning, either. No one has ever felt brave enough to hint to Humphrey that he'd get his manor fast enough if he'd take an Indian bride. He seems contented to be a bachelor and look after young George. . . . Ever since the women found out that his little book which Mark Bennet sneered at had household directions in it, too, he has been badgered to lend it. He deplored our lack of books in the beginning and as the years come and go, I wonder what our children will do, when the Latin is in tatters and all the prayer books worn. Am I wrong to be reconciled that little Cedric did not live, when I have no notion of what these other babes who survive him will find in years to come? My Betsey is well and hopes that our second child, to come in midsummer, will live.

Mark Bennet was confirmed last week. On the first Sunday of the New Year I shall read the banns for the first time for his marriage to Emma Merrimoth, the last of the spinsters. He hadn't much choice, but she did, which speaks well for his improved disposition. He seems reconciled now to having a place in our community only as our master carpenter. It was a great blight on his spirit for a long time that he wasn't more respected as a leader. But when the news came about John White's return and all the people learned the truth about their real relationship to the Patentees, the meetings became less exclusive. Mark is invited to sit with them occasionally but he doesn't go every time, I've noticed. Power has lost its flavor for him.

New Year's Eve, 1595

For crops, a woeful year, because of dry weather. We've had to scrape, Indians and colonists alike, for food for the animals that sustain us. The well went low and Humphrey's bathing pool in the stream shrank to half its size. Most of the nut harvest wasn't worth picking up this autumn. The worms got in. If it hadn't been for the extra quantity of dried fish Mary brought from the Sound in August, we mightn't have fared as well as we did. The Harvies' oldest gander died. He didn't like fish.

The best said, it gave us a change from our dull routine. The same food for breakfast, the same flowers in the gardens, except where Emma Bennet has tamed a few wild ones. She has a strange skill at it.

In October the tribe's old chief died. I do not think it was hunger. Now Mary rules. Nias told me that descent is often in the female line among some tribes. He seems to have completely recovered his well being, and resisted the famine time better than some. All in all, we have fared well. If only I could see the purpose in it.

Lady of Roanoke

We had beautiful twins in midsummer, Penelope and Peter, borne through the drought with no whimper from their mother. Plym Berry was our only other birth this year. Jane has healthy babies and she's a good mother, but very firm.

New Year's Eve, 1596

We shall eventually reach the place where the sight of a doublet is a rarity. Betsey has put my best one, a black with green and scarlet slashed sleeves, in the chest to keep for the children. They are now flourishing on Viccars' milk and corn porridge. This year we've had normal moisture and Humphrey and his men brought in their usual excellent crop so that we asked all the Indians to attend a feast after the ingathering. It seemed a success by the amount of food consumed. The deer are plump this season.

New Year's Eve, 1597

A double wedding this year and the first break away from our original company which took the trail together seven years ago. I've wondered when it would come. John Sampson and Billy Wythers, boys then, were twenty this year. They didn't like school and thanks to Humphrey they were able to learn a trade. Billy knows all that Mark Bennet can teach him about furniture making. John is as good as the best Indian in curing and tailoring deerskin. He made his wife's wedding garment. The boys married two girls from Mary's wide-branching family. They left the next day to help start another settlement in the west. John's father and Billy's uncle, George Martyn, and George's other younger nephew, Tommy Smart, went with them, besides a small company of Indians. I think Nias minded Sampson's going more than he let on, the first Patentee to leave. At the last minute, the week before the weddings, both the Chapmans and Colmans decided to go, too. Some dispute here, I think, but Margery Harvie gave them a pair of geese to take along. . . . That move gave us the Rectory and the Prats took the Chapmans' house. It doesn't seem possible that we were with the Dares so long. William is almost eight, as much a handful as ever, but going to school. Our babies are two and a half, now.

New Year's Eve, 1598

A most uneventful year. I often feel that we are in a spot where Time stands still. Except for the rising of the sun and its going down, and the change of the seasons—the Indians have five which they call the *budding of spring, maturing of maize, high-sun time* (summer), *leaf-falling time*, and *cold*—our days are much the same. We have no money. We need none. The people are not concerned about the rector's stipend because it doesn't exist. I get my family's share of the food-stuffs Humphrey raises and the spun wool. Mistress Tappan is indefatigable about the spinning and weaving.

The twins flourish.

New Year's Eve, 1599

I am sitting to write this at a beautiful new table that

Lady of Roanoke

Mark Bennet has finished for my study. He's been seasoning the walnut since the first year we came to this place. He keeps the men busy, which is healthy, but there is more time now for them to hunt and fish and play at bowls. Since Humphrey got the stream dredged and cleaned some very good fish have been taken from it. Mark was skeptical when the boy wanted tree branches lopped off above so that the sun could reach the water. But there is no more odor of decaying vegetation and one can see the bottom because it is so clean. Humphrey is a puzzling young man, altogether. He seems so contented just as he is, with no desire to marry. He comes in to read Greek with me occasionally, having exhausted my Latin books, and we talk. He and young George Howe are faring very well. All the colony women fuss and mother them. So their house is clean and they have a hot meal to their liking, and their shirts washed and mended. Humphrey is a natural-born father, as well as farmer. It seems such a waste there is no colony girl for him to wed.

New Year's Eve, 1600

We've lived one year in this century, this night. The twins are five-and-a-half and this morning my Betsey gave them a little sister, Mary Glane Brooke, no less. She looks like her mother and has my long frame. . . . We had a brief fright in the summer when Manteo had us all huddled in the Long House for a day and a half, because an ugly band of Tuscaroras, their mortal enemies, had been seen in the neighborhood. But nothing happened, and we were thankful to disperse to our homes again. The little Lady of Roanoke, no longer little, being now past her thirteenth birthday, and tall and lithe, went cantering out to Humphrey's house, not trusting anyone else to warn him. He's twenty-seven now, and her godfather, which I had almost forgot until her mother reminded me of it recently. We were talking about her reckless defiance of every convention, if she doesn't see him reasonably often. The child's devotion to him is a worrying thing, altogether. . . . We've heard from John and Billy. One of the Indians from their settlement came back for a visit. They are doing well. Both have started families.

VIRGINIA'S DILEMMA

18

The small Barbary horse though old was still sturdy, but had stopped hurrying, not even when returning to his stable, no matter how long he had been away from it.

This morning he was leaving his stall and his feet were hock deep in the golden leaves of October, a great flurry of them, fallen in last night's wind.

Virginia rode him astride, in a long, divided riding skirt of deerskin, to the shocked horror of the colony matrons. Getting it from her mother and Mary had been one of her more difficult victories in seventeen years of struggle to have her own way.

VIRGINIA'S DILEMMA

She prodded the Barbary with a hopeful, moccasined toe, never giving up. It would be fun to hear the
crisp swish and rustle of the leaves as he charged
through and one day he might surprise himself and her
and really go. This could be the time. But it wasn't.
Instead, he stopped so abruptly that she almost slid off
backwards.

"Hero! Come along. What a place to halt. There
aren't any nut trees here. You can't be tired. We've
barely begun. Oh, may a murrain seize you, Hero. No,
no, I wouldn't want that. But move!"

Humphrey had named the Barbary for her, out of
one of his Latin books and she had never understood
why. He wasn't a hero, never had been anything but
a sedate plodder. How she still longed to race across
the moor beyond the fields, away and away.

He was only a larger animal, no different from the
stubborn little pony the colony children had owned together, years ago. She hadn't been four, when the big
boys built a stable for it, and there it was, one morning
when she woke up. Her very own pony, that Mary
said she could have. And Humphrey wouldn't allow it.
He said I was selfish and he spanked me. Does everyone
remember when they were three or almost four? Or
do I, because it was Humphrey? I think I recall every
word he ever said to me. Oh, no, Virginia, you don't,
she chided. It's only because you are . . .

What *could* a girl do, she wondered desperately,
one who had been rocked in her cradle and later
spanked to aid her growing up, by a big boy who still

must think of her as a little sister, or his goddaughter, and not as a possible someone to love and to cherish . . . ? What? How?

She felt her face burning and put her hands up, and thus, because she had lifted her head she saw the moccasined foot beneath the bush opposite Hero's stubborn stand.

It wasn't fright that made her gasp. It didn't occur to her to be anything but angry. How dared . . . ?

But then the face appeared and the hands, cautiously parting the branches, and it was only Oppy, one of Manteo's many relatives, who had been with her in school. He thrust his way out of the bush without any embarrassment for waylaying her and stepped to Hero's head, bent and rubbed noses with him.

"This one will go now," he said. "He knows me and waited until I came out. He likes people to do this."

Virginia almost gaped. As long as she had known Hero, her own horse, not shared with anyone, she hadn't learned that. But Oppy could be showing off, too. Mayhap all the Barbary ponies owned by Mary and her people had been trained to expect a nose rub. Her jealous thought eased and when Oppy told her why he had come, would the White Fawn talk to him, she received it coolly.

"If it doesn't take too long, Oppy. I came out for a ride."

He said, "I want to be . . . I came to ask to be . . . how you say it, White Fawn? What your father is to the White Doe, your mother . . . that word?"

Virginia shook her head, not understanding, then light broke and she said, in dismay, "Oh, Oppy, you don't mean *husband*?"

"Oh, yes, yes. I want to be that. Those big boys, John and Billy, they married my sisters and took them away out there . . ." he waved his arm to take in generously the whole woods westward, on the blue hills, ". . . so, if you'd come marry with me, we could go to them. That I would like."

She wanted to cry, desperately, and couldn't understand why. She wished for Humphrey, too, in the same degree. He'd know what she should say. And that made her want to laugh.

But she mustn't hurt Oppy's feelings. She sat a moment, feeling Hero gathering himself as if he was ready to go on again. She had brought a basket, hoping to find a few nuts as proof that that had been her errand, when all she had wanted was to ride and think. Now there was Oppy.

What could she say? Oh, his age, of course. "Oppy, how old are you?"

He frowned and swallowed nervously. "The White Fawn means how many moons am I?"

She nodded, silently, not wanting to disturb his thought with more words.

He struggled with it and by use of his fingers made her understand it was sixteen years since he had been born on the Sound.

Virginia shook her head. "Not enough, Oppy. I have one more than yours. And it is our custom that the man—that would be you—must go to my father to say he wants to be my husband. And then my father will say that only one with many, many more moons than mine will be marrying with me."

"Not enough?" Oppy repeated, sadly. "But, White Fawn, you must listen to me. I have land, and ponies and my strong bow, and mats and . . ."

"They are not enough, Oppy. I am sorry. But you have given me great honor."

"Oh, do not say it, White Fawn."

"But I will say it." She pointed upward at the trees, so bare now that the sky shone through. "Yes, Oppy, honor that will last until the leaves come no more and the stars fade from the sky."

He must understand that. It was fanciful enough. The Indians themselves spoke in that fashion.

She seemed to have convinced him because he turned to go. He looked back at her once, mournfully, after he had gone a few paces, and then he disappeared along some quiet trail of his own.

Virginia slid off Hero's back and led him until they came to a nut tree with a respectable fallen crop, enough to fill her basket, which she did mechanically while thinking about the Indian lad and Humphrey and that other, recent, halting talk with Georgie Howe.

She hadn't turned her hand, much less smiled provokingly at him or Oppy. If only someone would tell her the way to make Humphrey . . . what if he *was* fourteen when she was born? Seventeen years ago, and a bit . . . mid-August to October, for that.

VIRGINIA'S DILEMMA

Jane Pierce. Elizabeth Glane. Jane Mannering. Emma Merrimoth. What had they done that she couldn't do? How to find out? The colony women still loved to talk about the cambric petticoat given so mysteriously for Roger Prat's vestments and how it turned out to be from Jane Mannering, because she had got acquainted with him while teaching in the school together. And the way Betsey had got her wedding gown ready before the rector had even asked her to be a-marrying with him. Where had she got her faith?

Hero was turned around and Virginia climbed on his back and held the basket carefully while he went home at his own gait with never a cluck nor a toe prod the whole way in to his sapling pole stable.

Virginia was very quiet at table during the noon meal and didn't argue once with William—gave her parents the impression, indeed, that she didn't know what she was eating and didn't care.

After Virginia went to her room and William to his class, Ananias worried to Eleanor that the girl must be sickening for something.

Eleanor said, "It's a sickness all right and she's already got it, the kind that Humphrey Hall could cure, an he'd ask her to marry him. Can't you do something, Nias? Now that she's a young lady and doesn't go to school any more, he thinks he's raised a pretty good crop and is letting her be. She misses the scoldings and the . . . the . . . Nias, don't look so."

"Humphrey Hall!" he exclaimed. "He's so much

older. Now if it was Georgie . . . They're nearer a like age."

"But Nias, she's followed Humphrey around all her life. She learned it early, because he was always . . . well, just *there* when she needed someone, and you were so busy with the colony business. You think back on it. He's a little serious but a good lad and no better stock in Yorkshire."

"I'd get her the moon, an I could, Eleanor. But get Humphrey to wed her, that I cannot do, an he does not ask me to. It was done that way when we were young in England, but not here, Eleanor, not here."

"She rides and roams and broods, and it isn't wholesome. That could sicken her, by itself. I've tried teaching her to cook, but she will have none of it."

"That's lack of gumption," said Ananias. "Humphrey likes his victuals. . . . I *can* talk to Brooke."

"The last one to ask, Nias, for the kind of advice we need. He didn't know what hit him until long after it struck. And Betsey with her wedding gown made and waiting. And I, worrying. You do some now, Nias."

He grinned and went away and Virginia passed through the kitchen, dressed still in her riding skirt, saying she was going over to see Mistress Betsey, with the nuts gathered for the children.

"Ask her to let me borrow the needle? If Margery Harvie hasn't got it? I can finish off three more rush mats an I may have it. Your father wears out one a week on the front door stone."

VIRGINIA'S DILEMMA

The needle was a sharp-pointed fish bone, polished to ivory smoothness and appearance from years of use. It took a long time to wear one down to such perfection and the colony women handled it almost reverently, for sewing skins and rushes. Mary had promised another but there was only one bone like that in each fish from the Sound and her women had need, too.

It was safe for one more time, because Virginia forgot it, as soon as she was on Hero's back. The basket was heavy and the Rectory lay on the far side of the green.

Betsey was giving her youngest his bath and the twins and Mary were gathered round watching him gurgle and splash in the big earthen bowl, set on a bench in front of the open fire. He was aged eight months, just, Master Richard Grenville Brooke, but he looked older and acted so, too, yelling angrily when his mother lifted him out of the water.

"A proper baby loves his bath," Betsey remarked calmly, above the noise, "and he has to wait to this hour of the day, for the children to see. No time in the morning before school."

And then she saw the odd, pinched look on Virginia's face and reminded her family of their gift. "Go and find the pounding stone and crack some, or do a nice game outdoors, then? Don't bother your father, mind, he's making a sermon."

They were an obedient three, but they went reluctantly, looking back from the doorway at Virginia and their mother and the baby.

So Virginia said, "Hero is out there, waiting for

me. Mayhap you'd like to put Mary up and lead him home? On your way to school? I can walk back because I'll not have the basket."

"Oh, yes, thank you, we would," said Peter and they scampered away.

"How good they are," she said to Betsey. "They didn't want to go. I'd have howled at either of their ages."

"You did, often," said Betsey. "Enough to try a saint."

"I'd like to try one now. I could howl with rage this minute." Then, abruptly, "Why did you come to Roanoke?"

Betsey gave her a sharper look and said, "Oh, that's a bit of a tale. Let me put the baby down and rid up this clutter, there's a good girl. If John should come in . . . he likes a neat house."

She mended the fire when she came back, before she sat down. "With four to do for . . ." she waved an expressive hand at the large, comfortable room, "men are the blindest creatures, wanting it kept well, but not turning a hand . . . Yet we love'm. Is that your trouble, child? Came to Betsey with it, did you, like a sore finger, or a scratched knee? Not that you had many of those, with your long skirts, like a little woman. Melt any man's heart, that sight would, the only one in the colony then. Well Virginia, I've been looking for a visit from you."

Virginia exclaimed, "How could you tell?"

Betsey laughed. "Quieter than you used to be. No

pranks, lately. Anyway, it's natural. Seventeen is marrying time in England, why not here? Who's it? Georgie,
I suppose. You could do worse. Not Manteo? He's a
fine . . .'"

Virginia shook her head.

"No? Then who, give me grace to hear?"

When the tears fell, which Virginia couldn't hold
back, Betsey kindly rambled on, to give her a chance
to recover.

"You asked how I happened to come. Just one
reason, girl, to be marrying with somebody I'd like
better than the moldy ancient and his money that my
brother decided on for me. Mayhap your mother
hasn't said, but that's a spinster's fate in England, has
she no parents, to abide by a brother's choice. So when
I heard about the colony building up, I did a little in-
quiring, took my mother's family name and left for
Plymouth. They never traced me, and that's always
been a miracle to me, like Providence-meant. And first
off comes aboard the ship this tall, quiet person, and I
marked him out for mine."

"And it was the rector?" Virginia quavered.

"John Brooke, bless the creature. It took a while,
most three years, oh, more than that, but it came about
like the spots in fevers, when once they start."

"But, Betsey, that doesn't help me. I thought you'd
tell me something that, an it works for one, it does for
all. Humphrey's been spanking me and brothering me
all my life and his vision for a wife is veiled."

"So it's Humphrey? I wouldn't have thought . . .

Lady of Roanoke

well, mayhap I might, an I was still under the Dare
roof. He's not quite old enough to be your father. I'll
have to dwell on it a little, Virginia. But you won't
have to wait three years, an your heart's set on him.
He'll come to his senses, the way most men do. Sometimes a little late, there's my John for the prize of all.
Something'll stir Humphrey, and he'll be as surprised
as any, say what they may. There, little Lady of Roanoke, don't cry."

It was a long walk across the green, on the path
that connected all the houses, but Virginia had to do
only part of it alone.

Her heart almost stopped when she saw Humphrey
coming toward her in great strides—and if ever she had
seen him angrier, she didn't recall the time. There was
no one in sight, though every chimney had a smoke
pillar above it, in the lovely quiet of the October day.

"Now what's toward?" he called, as soon as he
knew she could hear, without a shout. "Virginia, how
you do try me. Come, let's go to the Looking Seat. Not
that I want to gaze at the hills today. Your face is more
to my notion so I can see what's behind this latest
caper. An you weren't seventeen, by Heaven, I'd be of
a mind to spank you."

"Never again, Humphrey Hall," said Virginia
crisply, "and there's no caper to set you into such a
taking. I vow not."

"You'll vow something to me, an I get the straight
of this. Here am I with the men at the pumpkins, laying

them by, so that we'll have good victualing in the cold, and I have to leave it to settle Oppy's wits. You've got him *so* addled, Virginia, it took me an hour, and still not untangled and the men hard-put to work, for laughing."

"Not at Oppy, an they heard him. Of humor there was none. I needed you to tell me what was proper to say. But you weren't there, so I had to think of something myself. There was nothing addling in it, either."

Humphrey listened and looked down into the lovely mournful eyes and had an absurd wish to kiss the girl. It was a different feeling from any he had had before, toward her, and it was pleasant. If only, long ago, he hadn't consented to be her godfather. If only, later, a little, innocent boy who had become almost as dear to him as this child before him, had not laid first claim to her, as wife. This present matter was now changed to something different from a big-brother scold. The men could be laughing at *him*, then, and not Oppy? What *had* Virginia told the boy? He must have that straight before he . . . before . . . no, he couldn't say a word. There was Georgie to think about, too.

It was difficult, therefore, to hold to the stern look when he said, "What did you tell Oppy this morning? He went home and stirred up the whole village so that Manteo brought him to me with it."

Virginia's hands were busy, tangling the fringe on the bottom of her jacket. Her heart was hammering and she was somehow afraid to look at Humphrey, his tone had so changed. Would he . . . ? She raised her head and fixed on a point in the far blue distance when she answered.

"The talk was not my seeking, Humphrey. He waylaid me in the path when I went to the nut trees this morning. I'm just back from giving a basket full to the Brooke children. They are such good young ones, Humphrey. You might have seen them, leading Hero home?

"Never mind the Brookes. What did you and Oppy talk about?"

"Humphrey, you've no call to get in a pucker about anything I say or that is said to me. Little enough you've bothered lately, and now you . . ."

"Go on, and I think you'd better look at me. I'm not in a pucker. I don't know what to call that which I'm in . . . and I can't believe you'd tell Oppy anything like his report of it."

And then she was in his arms, childhood fashion, sobbing it out and being soothed as she had been, all her life.

"I don't know what you mean. You make it sound awful. He wanted to be a-marrying with me, Humphrey, and he said we'd go where John and Billy and his sisters went. I told you I didn't know what to say. So, when I found he is only sixteen, I said he should go to my father and he would tell him that I wouldn't . . . it'd be only with a man many, many moons older, I'd be wed to. Your name wasn't even spoken, so you *are* in a taking, all for nothing, Humphrey Hall."

"No, because Oppy misunderstood you. There was something about his honor, too."

Virginia leaned back against the strong circle of his arms and clasped hands and wiped her tears away with the end of her jacket, but they would keep coming, though she tried to laugh at the strange look on Humphrey's face. He kept smoothing her hair but saying nothing.

"It's very hard to be the only girl of my years in this colony, Humphrey. You wouldn't guess the half of it. There was Georgie last week, asking me, too."

"So he finally did it!" Humphrey exclaimed, feeling some of his burden lift yet scarcely realizing it. "And wasn't he old enough either? He told me at the full age of eight that he meant to marry with you some day." He laughed at the memory, all his sternness gone. "And within an hour, you two were quarreling primely over a black puppy, all his good intentions forgot."

Virginia smiled, though not remembering. Not even tears were bringing Humphrey to his senses, though she hadn't called them forth at will. They just came, because everything looked so hopeless. But he hadn't taken his arms away. That was a little comforting, to have no change in what she had always had.

So she said, mildly, "The thing I said to Oppy about honor was what I thought he'd understand the most."

"But he didn't. And to begin with he was most woefully hurt because you said he wasn't old enough."

"Oh, Humphrey you should have been there."

"Had I been, little goose, it wouldn't have happened. I am beginning to see, a little, how this whole matter might be my fault. Oppy seems meek, but he rather fancies his looks, and his possessions, and that one year of difference in your ages was only pish and tush to him. And then to take his honor away. Oh, Virginia, how could you?"

"A murrain take him," said Virginia. "What can he have thought?"

"He said you wanted an old, old man to be wed with, which was bad enough, amounting to an insult. But you took his honor away as well and you said he'd never get it back until the leaves stop growing on the trees and there were no more stars."

"Humphrey, he couldn't."

"But he did, little lady, and now we have to find a way to give it back to him. Manteo will know how when he learns the truth of it. What did you mean?"

"I was trying to tell him that he had paid me honor for asking me to marry with him and that I'd never forget it for that long."

"Very pretty manners, and it is too bad that it was all lost for Oppy. He needs to learn some more English. You might be the teacher."

"Humphrey!"

He loosed one hand to smooth her curls back from her flushed face and settle her cap, in such an accustomed fashion that neither noticed it. Then he smiled benignly and startled her by his very calm when he said, "You need me to look after you now, quite as much as you ever did. Do you think, dear little Lady of Roanoke, that I might be that old man—the one you described to Oppy this morning? Born so many, many moons before you? To be wed with, to love and to cherish, the way it goes in the prayer book? If Oppy is too young, and Georgie not enough older, would I do?"

Virginia flung herself with a thump against Humphrey's chest and rested her head beneath his chin where she had been snuggled too many times to count, when she was sleepy, or tired or cross or all three, and her arms circled his neck.

"Oh Humphrey, I thought you'd never say it. That's what I've been trying to tell you, all this while. You're right slow, most a match for the rector."

"Then you don't mind having an old man of thirty-one for your husband, who is also your god-father?"

"If that's all has kept you . . . Oh, Humphrey, I'm *so* happy."

Margery Harvie could see directly across the green with nothing to obstruct her view, as Mark Bennet had planned when he placed the houses, and when she saw the two on the Looking Seat *in the mid-afternoon and the pumpkin harvest on, of all times,* she reached for her cap and ran over to the rectory with the needle though she wasn't quite through with it.

The whole colony had the news for its supper tables.

EXODUS

19

By autumn of the year 1608, Humphrey had been married to Virginia for four years. Her tempers had not abated, rather, the old childish ways of getting what she wanted were giving place to mature discussion. She had borne a son, Andrew Dare Hall, now a lusty lad of two. They were happy.

Colonists and Indians alike were doing well, though their young were restive.

Humphrey was still chief planter, and the crops he raised had become routine. So he welcomed Roger Prat's experiments for diversion. Just then, in a separate small plot they had some plants bearing round red fruit that was palatable though many were suspicious that the little love apples were poison, because they belonged to a botanical family Roger identified as a nightshade. No one had yet died of it.

Sheep cropped the grass in Humphrey's wide dooryard. There were still little flowers in it, as on that first day in 1590 when other grass had been crushed by knees bent to pray.

The stream where fine fish could now be caught, hadn't yet, after eighteen years, worn away the stones it babbled over down in the valley.

Three of the birthday gold sovereigns Humphrey had saved long ago, to bring to the New World, were still in his possession. The amethyst ring was too large for Virginia's finger but she wore it anyway, wrapped round with a thread of homespun to make it stay on.

Humphrey himself was restive along with the new generation growing up. Eighteen years and he still hadn't been given his manor. The land he worked on, tilled, improved, belonged to the tribe as it always had.

It hadn't taken long after his wedding with Virginia to see the truth. His marriage had put the seal on it. Why had he been so innocent, perhaps a little arrogant, in accepting Manteo's assurance that he could hope for his own farm, in the face of tribal law and custom? He couldn't name the hour, the minute, the day when he first began to see the pattern.

He was only more sure after that first week of his marriage, that it had been in Manteo's mind to bind the colonists to the tribe by an irrevocable link—an older girl of his family for Humphrey to wife, and Oppy growing up with Virginia in school, to be ready to marry her, when the time came. That was part of the reason why the Corees had been so ready to respond to the colonists' invitation, so tardily given, to include their children in the school.

It wasn't cruel or selfish. It was only the Indian way of thought, not understandable in some areas by any Englishman, and indeed the more deeply desired by the Corees because of the friendships established first at Roanoke.

They were definitely pleased when Georgie asked to marry Felicity, Manteo's little sister. And, as the pattern unrolled in Humphrey's mind, it explained how much more was involved than Oppy's own feelings of hurt pride the day he had risked his future by speaking to Virginia before Manteo was ready for the proposal to be made. That was why his concern and apology at the time had seemed greater than necessary. He had probably been hoping for another double ceremony, such as the one celebrated for John and Billy and their Indian brides, and if it couldn't yet be Humphrey with a wife from the tribe, Virginia and Oppy could have been the other couple, when Georgie and Felicity were married, a further lure for Humphrey to follow their example.

Nias had recognized the pattern long ago, but it was only after Virginia's betrothal and marriage to Humphrey that he had reluctantly confirmed his son-in-law's awakened understanding of Manteo's well-meant, even loving intent. Poor Manteo!

EXODUS

One bright autumn noonday, close to his wedding anniversary, Humphrey sat on the porch of his house—the only one in the colony built that way—and played with young Andrew while waiting for the midday meal. It was to be a splendid great fish caught that morning and already the fragrance of the broiling was rich in the air.

Between one glance and the next at the laughing child Humphrey was tossing so expertly, he was aware of three who came out of the woods to the north where the Indian village lay, and took the path to his door-yard.

One was Manteo and the other two were white men, bearded, who from their looks had been several days a-journeying.

Humphrey's heart jolted, but not from fear of danger. Manteo's presence meant that the strangers' mission was peaceful. But he hadn't seen another Englishman, save his own colonist neighbors, since he had first landed on Roanoke.

Manteo said, "These *would* come," which was his apology for allowing it.

Humphrey couldn't detect any clue to the visit on Manteo's face nor that of either man, though they had got through the protective barrier of the Indian village, where they would have had to give some reason plausible enough to be permitted to come this far.

What could it mean? Until that moment the Roanoke people thought they were the only Englishmen on the mainland. Humphrey set the little boy down, gave him a gentle push toward the house door and

called for one of Virginia's young Indian maids to come
for the child. When Andrew was safely gathered in,
he stood above the single step, a roughhewn stone,
which led to the porch, and waited for the three to
come close enough for further speech.

The strangers' hands lay carelessly on the muskets
they carried, quite like those still remaining good, in
the colony.

Humphrey hid his apprehension under a lazy grin.
"I will hear what they have to say. Bide, Manteo."

The elder of the two men, and neither was old,
had looked Humphrey over, missing little, by the time
he reached the stone. He said now, bluntly, "Your
Indian friends weren't sure of our welcome here."

"And you think they should have been sure?"

"An you have nothing to hide, yes," said the
visitor. "Easy enough manner, they had, else. Corees
by the look. Clean Indian folks. Liked'm." He turned
to his companion and raised his brows in question.

"Did," the other agreed.

Whether calculated or not, it was the best possible
thing to say, to insure being invited in and fed.

As they stepped up onto the stone, the younger
man sniffed and remarked, "Good cookin' here, seems."

"Fish," said Humphrey, turned as terse as they.
"Bide. You won't need your guns."

"Name of Scitmore," said the elder, then, tapping
his chest. "He's Rollins."

Both men looked at Humphrey and waited for a
like revelation and Manteo watched.

EXODUS

Humphrey thought swiftly. It hadn't occurred to him before, because he had never imagined such a situation, that his house might appear as an isolated farmstead. The colony dwellings were all hidden by trees to the south. But these two Englishmen had seen him and the Indians. They could draw what conclusions they liked, but a report of some kind could go to England and embarrassing questions could ensue, and eventually the whole story would come out. Why hadn't they maintained a watch on the coast if they felt they must come inland, so that an English ship might be hailed?

He cleared his throat and asked a delaying question. "What brings you here, sirs? Your are trail weary and your clothes . . ." he spread his hand to include both the state of their garments and their rough beards.

The spokesman looked at the younger, who nodded. So he said, "Instructions, some. Kindness, too. And a little curiosity added. We been hearin' of men dressin' like us and not so far away, for a year's time. Indian gossip. Now our Captain's had an order from England to look for the Raleigh colony, lost since 1587. Story goes they ain't been seen or heard of since John White went back to England on the ship that brought'm. He was to bring some goods on return."

Humphrey's breathing quickened. "But it's been twenty years. Surely he hasn't come now? He must be quite an old man. But perhaps he has sent . . . we could use . . ."

Scitmore's pleased grin made him realize the significance of what he had said. He smiled in return and spread his hands wide. They could often speak more eloquently for him than his tongue. "I'm Humphrey Hall from York. I was a Roanoke colonist, as I've just shown."

"No such name on the ship's list," Scitmore objected.

H'm. They were well posted for their errand. It somehow proved their bona fides.

Humphrey said, "Oh, but I was there, my name only in part on the list. Didn't you see Thomas Humfrey? That was the way I signed when I wrote Sir Walter. The Dares were my family's neighbors. I wanted to come to the New World and Mistress Dare encouraged it. Fourteen years old, I was, wanting to be a farmer, and so I am."

Scitmore nodded, accepting the explanation as reasonable.

"Who is your captain?" Humphrey asked. "Where are you settled? See, the food is coming. Virginia, these strangers are hungry. Mistress Hall was Virginia Dare, first white child born in this part of the New World. We can talk while we eat. I should like her to hear your story. Manteo, sit here."

If the men had told Manteo a different one, now it would appear, Humphrey thought.

He himself had turned interrogator. That should help.

A little maid brought more plates. They ate with their fingers, using bread to coax the last drops of juice from the tender white flakes of the big fish.

EXODUS

Scitmore said, "Best meal we've had in days, eh, Rollins? Our story's easy told. We're from a colony settled last year on the James River—Jamestown—named for the king. It's north of here, twelve leagues, thereabout."

"King?" Humphrey questioned. He turned to Virginia. "Elizabeth was our queen when you were born. She must have died."

"Yes, five years gone," said Scitmore. "News, eh? And they got the Scots' Jamie to come down to Lunnon and they crowned him James I." He screwed his face up and added, "A little fellow. Things are different now, from a woman's rule."

Humphrey said, "I hadn't realized how much things could change in a few years. I was still growing up when we came here. And all were so pressed to keep alive—food and shelter—the time has passed, somehow . . ."

"Reasonable," said Scitmore, interrupting briskly. "Now ye're found, what's to do? Any more of you round and about? Might like to know Sir Walter's in the Tower, probably there to stay until . . ." he shrugged. "John White is dead, leastways no one's heard of him since 1593. Their scores with you seem settled."

Humphrey said, thoughtfully, "What good will come of our being found, now? Yes, there are others, still here, who felt it good to disappear, at the time of our leaving Roanoke. *Must* you report this visit? Put yourselves in our places."

Lady of Roanoke

Scitmore looked at Rollins. He looked at Scitmore. No words sounded but they decided to be
compassionate.

"No, no need to report it, if'n that's what you
want. Can't give you any guarantee, though. Have to
trust that we won't, is all."

"It's not for me alone to say, of course. Our Patentees are still our authority here, by the consent of the
people, for matters that concern all. This does, truly.
Nine came from Roanoke. Seven are left. Bide over
until this matter may be talked of in fair speech, with
all present."

Rollins looked at Scitmore, who said, "Wouldn't
do to get back to Jamestown too soon. Captain'd think
we hadn't done our errand, maybe didn't get this far,
if we get back too soon. And there's the added per-
suasion of the good cookin' in these parts, an today's
fish a sample. Guess we'll bide, Rollins, and thank ye,
kindly, sir."

The next day at evening, Humphrey sat on his
porch again, soothing Andrew to sleep. The little boy
must be aware of the excited atmosphere since the
arrival of the two strangers. He was refusing to settle.

The colonists' decision to send the strangers off
without a report, leaving it to them what they'd say
on their return to Jamestown, was not a surprise to
Humphrey. The more that the man Scitmore told of
changes at home, the surer they were that life in the
greenwood was better for them. Why be found? It
had lost its significance one way or the other.

Things never stayed the same, anywhere, Humphrey mused, as he gently rubbed Andrew's back. He had found it a good method to soothe a child, first with Georgie and then Virginia. His hand was practiced now.

Eighteen years they'd been in this inland place. Long enough for the first babies born hereabout to be thinking of their own marriages. The rector's Peter, at almost-fourteen, was already showing a farming bent. And the banns for Little Amby and Megan Jones had been read the third time last Sabbath. Amby was twenty-three now and still plump, Megan at eighteen a blue-eyed dark-haired beauty, as much of a minx as the little Lady of Roanoke had ever thought of being.

"Can you make me a cambric shirt?" he hummed, remembering the sleeping babe in the basket at Tom's feet on a long-ago morning. No, not a shirt, and neither a manor. He hadn't been able to make one, without legal Indian ownership, any better than the original shirt maker without a needle.

He looked up and there was Georgie coming across the grass, followed by his silent, devoted little Felicity, who held their firstborn, another Mary.

Humphrey called Virginia and she came and lifted Andrew and she and Felicity disappeared, leaving their husbands settled to tobacco, colony grown and cured.

It was a full half hour before Georgie spoke his errand. "Little Amby and Megan want to go to that place where John and Billy went. There is a good road. And Felicity and I would like to go, if you . . . d' you think it would be all right, Humphrey? We wouldn't

be cutting ourselves off from . . . from the colony. It's
the way Little Amby says, we do the same things over
and over, every day, here. Out there . . ." he nodded
vaguely westward, "we'd have it new . . . we were
children when we came here. Everything was done for
us. There we'd have to do . . . whatever is needed . . .
ourselves. An we stayed here, I'd have my own land,
through Felicity . . . that was the reason you never got
your manor, Humphrey. I s'pose you've known long
since . . . I'd like . . ."

He was startled to hear the farmer say, as he rose,
abruptly, knocking his chair over, "D'ya mind if old
man Hall brings his family, too? Let's go talk to the
wives. I've been thinking the same as you. Plenty of
men left here can do the crops as well as I have."

Georgie laughed. "That's what we came for. Oh,
Humphrey, we couldn't have left you . . ."

They met the girls in the door.

Virginia's eyes were glowing and her face flushed.
She said, "Humphrey, can't we go, too? If mamma will
let me take the cradle?"

Humphrey groaned. He could see himself, after all
the years, taking the trail again with it on his back. But
of course this time they'd have a Barbary or so to help.

After the Howes had gone, he sat a while on the
porch alone. The crickets and the stream in the valley
and the soft night-wind stirring the tops of the pine
trees were whispering one refrain, over and over—it
was bound to come, to come, to come, bound to.

EPILOGUE

The chief reason for Governor White's long delay in returning to Roanoke Island was the troubled time he found in England when he arrived there in November of 1587. The threat of Spain's invasion by sea kept every English ship in home waters. All the famous captains—Grenville, Drake, Frobisher and Hawkins and many a lesser one—were rallying. Yet in April of 1588, John White prevailed upon Sir Walter Raleigh to procure special license for two small vessels to sail for Roanoke. They were compelled to return after six weeks at sea because of critical disabling in enemy encounters.

The Spanish Armada reached Plymouth in July

1588, where it engaged the English ships in a great sea battle. Only half of the Spanish fleet was able to return to their home ports.

In March of 1589 Sir Walter Raleigh assigned or leased all his interest in Roanoke colony to Thomas Smith (afterwards knighted), John White and others, thus relinquishing his active interest in New World projects, though Governor White continued to beg for supplies and relief for *the planters in Virginia.*

Later, based on the knowledge that a merchant of London wanted to send three ships to the West Indies, John White again prevailed on Sir Walter to obtain a special license, though another general embargo was then current on all ports and shipping because Spain, in spite of the Armada's defeat, continued to threaten England.

Eventually, Governor White sailed in 1591, without the hoped-for provisions, arriving at Roanoke in August, with the results he reported to Richard Hakluyt in 1593.

Afterward, during a period of about fifteen years, there were several other relief attempts financed by Sir Walter Raleigh on behalf of the Roanoke colonists, which failed uniformly, because, historians say, the search was not systematic and didn't go far enough. The captains were more interested in booty they might snatch from a stray Spanish ship in the Carribbean.

Then, in May of 1607, Christopher Newport, under patent to the Virginia Company—headed by Sir Thomas Smith—founded a colony at the mouth of the James

River in Virginia. The following year he received orders to search for the colonists *last heard of in 1587.*

In *A True and Sincere Declaration,* dated December 1609, made by the governor and councilors of the Jamestown Colony, there is mention of the presence of some people thought to be the 1587 colonists within fifty miles of their own location. But there is no recorded evidence that anyone at Jamestown ever saw *the men who dress as we do* and who, according to Indian reports, *live in stone houses of two storeys.* The reason given was that *the savages denied them speech* with the explorers sent to find them.

There is a legend, among many about the Lost Colony, that the famous Indian Chief, Powhatan, angered by the arrival of more white men when Jamestown was settled, indulged in a sweeping massacre which was thought to include some settlements where Raleigh's people were assumed to be living, from which a few escaped.

But the Corees had won a reputation as a migratory people and they had many roots all over the eastern seaboard which became North and South Carolina in time. The inevitable intermarriage would increase numbers in any one location, and the wanderings to make other settlements seem reasonable.

The spot where the colonists are first supposed to have settled on leaving Roanoke could have been the *pleasant bluffs of Bertie County* (in present-day North Carolina), fifty miles inland, those goodly highlands where the Indians already had planted cornfields. Mi-

gration westward led to several settlements near the
Black River in what is now Sampson County. Some
went as far as Cape Fear in the south, believed to be
the original seat of the Hatteras-Coree-Algonquins.
Others went northwest from Cape Fear and reached the
Pee Dee River just inside the eastern border of modern
South Carolina.

There is physical proof that they survived for some
time thereafter in the fact that today, in Robeson
County, North Carolina, which lies just across the
state line from South Carolina there are people of mixed
English and Indian blood who have no memory of a
tribal language, whose surnames are those of noted
Raleigh colonists—the ship's roster was preserved and
is available to historians in several places—and who, in
this twentieth century, casually use obsolete English
words in their everyday speech. And, without excep-
tion their family traditions go back unerringly and
together, to Roanoke, in tangible proofs and orally,
that the people of Sir Walter Raleigh's Lost Colony
were their forbears. Family names and family tales
handed down, as families have done since the first
parents. Records of marriages. Deeds to property granted to a later generation of Berrys by King George II
in 1732. Enough to lead historians to believe that the
Dares, the Viccars, the Berrys and Chapmans and others
came to the mainland of what is now North Carolina
and there lived an allotted life span in the wilderness
they conquered and bent to their needs, learning from
the Indians and teaching them in return, an advantage
to all. Intermarriage was almost inevitable.

EPILOGUE

Another Robeson County colonial name is still prominent, though it was not on the roster of the Raleigh colonists who first settled on Roanoke. The association of the *Lowrie* family with the descendants of Henry Berry, Roanoke colonist, is notable here for reasons that will appear.

In 1690 one James Lowrie, Irishman, was appointed as His Majesty's Judge at Hampton, Virginia. He there married a Tuscarora princess. They had three sons and two daughters.

James Lowrie, Jr., born in 1710, received a grant of land from King George II (1727–1760, his reign) in 1732, in partnership with *Henry Berry*, descendant of that other Henry Berry who was a Roanoke colonist. The land in the grant was located in Robeson County and became known as the Lowrie Swamp, near the Lumber River, a tributary of the Pee Dee. Later, James Lowrie, Jr., was married to Priscilla Berry, sister of his partner, Henry.

The deed to the two young men, and a later one, dated in 1738, made separately to James by the same George, still exist.

Communication was important to the migratory Corees and their English friends and relatives, so they became skilled road builders. The most famous one, still in use after two hundred years, called Lowrie Road, connects Fayetteville in Cumberland County, N. C., with the old Coree settlement on the Pee Dee River in South Carolina.

Besides the good fortune the colonists had in the friendliness of Manteo's people, the climate of the country inland was favorable for the preservation of at least some of the original company.

North Carolina is in the central belt of the temperate zone. Its winters are not severe and summers are not oppressive, even in the low country. Ice rarely forms from the Blue Ridge mountains to the seaboard. From October to December there is, according to a North Carolina Government Report from its Department of Agriculture, an almost uninterrupted succession of bright sunny days, with dry air, crisp and pure. First frosts can be expected about mid-October.

There was also fresh water, and wild food in plenty in the forests. This was attested a hundred years later by John Lawson, who was a Surveyor-General of North Carolina at the time, which took him traveling about the state for eight years. In a journal he kept he mentions *turkies*, venison and vast flocks of pigeons, which were clubbed from roosting places in trees, flocks so numerous that they darkened the sky when they flew. These could have been the famous passenger pigeons, which are now extinct.

These details have emerged from patient explorings into oral tradition, legend and ancient memory, and private journals made into a mosaic of bits and pieces that is coastal history of the United States.

Placing the Dare family in Yorkshire for origin is historical. The name was originally spelled *Dayre* in England, was written Dare on the ship's list, and has come down in North Carolina as Dorr or Durr, the spelling yielding to pronunciation, probably. The name

EPILOGUE

Dare—Dorr—or Durr seems to have disappeared after the War of 1812.

The names of the characters in the story have been taken from the original list of colonists, men, women and children. The identity of *Thomas Humfrey* with the fictional Humphrey Hall is developed in the tale.

The birth of succeeding children are my writer's privileged conception, logically filling in the gaps of genealogical lines because they had to exist if the names of their families were to be carried on to modern times, as some have been.

For myself, I accept existing proof that descendants of the Dares and other Raleigh colonists still live and work in North Carolina. I have visited in Robeson County, have talked with members of those families and have no doubt at all that this theory of the later whereabouts of Sir Walter's people is more than probable. It's logical.

Why?

An ace up my sleeve. Look at the record of colonization, the dates. Roanoke, 1587. Jamestown, 1607. Twenty years between. It was not until 1609 that an emigrant colony from Jamestown settled in northeastern North Carolina. *It means that Sir Walter's lost Englishmen and women were the only colonists on the eastern coast at that period and with those names, who could have qualified as ancestors of present-day Americans. The generations wouldn't work out on any family tree, else.*

Was Fate in it? Was the Spanish Armada the sinister agent? Or, were all the happenings that stemmed from the Raleigh colonists' sojourn on Roanoke Island, bound to come, bound to be?

Let Sir Francis Bacon have the final word. In his essay, *Of Plantations,* he says:

It is the sinfullest thing in the world to forsake or destitute a plantation once in forwardness; for besides the dishonour, it is the guiltiness of blood of many commiserable persons.

BIBLIOGRAPHY

Baldwin, Thos. W.

William Shakspere's Petty School. Urbana: University of Illinois Press, 1943.

Binyon, Laurence

English Water Colours. London: A. & C. Black, 1933.

Busk, Hans

The Rifle and How to Use It. London: Routledge, Warne & Routledge, 1861.

Byrne, M. St. Clare

Elizabethan Life in Town and Country. New York: Barnes and Noble; London: Methuen, 1925 (reissue, 1961).

Davis, William Stearns

Life in Elizabethan Days. New York: Harper & Brothers, 1930.

Department of Agriculture Bulletin

North Carolina, A General Sketch of its Surface, Climate, Productions, Institutions, etc. Raleigh, 1886.

Lady of Roanoke

Gardner, Robert Edward — *Five Centuries of Gunsmiths, Swordsmiths and Armourers, 1400–1900*. Columbus, Ohio: Walter F. Herr, Publisher, 1948.

Hakluyt, Richard — *Explorations, Descriptions and Attempted Settlements of North Carolina, 1584–1590*. Raleigh, North Carolina: State Department of Archives and History, 1948.

Hawks, Francis L. — *History of North Carolina, Volume II, 1663–1729*. Fayetteville, North Carolina: E. J. Hale & Son, 1858.

Haydn, Hiram (ed.) — *Elizabethan Readers* New York: Viking, 1946.

Lorant, Stefan — *The New World, The First Pictures of America, made by John L. White and Jacques Le Moyne and engraved by Theodore De Bry*. New York: Duell, Sloan & Pearce, 1946.

Prayer Books

The Book of Common Prayer. According to the use of the Protestant Episcopal Church (Preface and Ordination sections).

The Book of Common Prayer, Church of England. Printed by Whitechurch, March, 1559 (William Pickering, London, 1844).

BIBLIOGRAPHY

Rowse, A. L. — *The England of Elizabeth.* New York: Macmillan, 1951.

—— — *Expansion of Elizabethan England.* New York: St. Martin's, 1955.

—— — *Sir Walter Raleigh, His Family and Private Life.* New York: Harper & Brothers, 1962.

United States Senate — *Document No. 677, The Indians of North Carolina, A Report.* Washington, D.C.: Government Printing Office, 1915.

Weeks, Stephen B. — *Papers of the American Historical Association* (Vol. 5). New York: Knickerbocker Press, 1891.

Wheeler, John H. — *Historical Sketches of North Carolina, 1584–1851.* Philadelphia: J. B. Lippincott, 1851.

Williamson, Hugh — *The History of North Carolina* (2 Vol.). Philadelphia: Thomas Dobson, 1812.

Magazine Articles

Amsden, Charles Avery. "The Loom and Its Prototypes," *American Anthropologist,* 34 (1932), 216-235.

Cummings, William Patterson. "The Identity of John White, Governor of Roanoke and John White Artist," *North Carolina Review,* 15 (July 1938), 197–203.

Epler, Blanch Nettleton. "A Bit of Elizabethan England in America," *The National Geographic*, December 1933.

Guild, Eugene R. "Exploring America's Great Sand Barrier Reef," *The National Geographic*, September 1947.

Jones, Stuart E. "Indian Life before the Colonists Came," *The National Geographic*, September 1947.

Stirling, Matthew W. "America's First Settlers," *The National Geographic*, November 1937.

ABOUT THE AUTHOR

Jean Bothwell, author of over forty books for young people, was an avid reader of history as a child and majored in that field at Nebraska Wesleyan University—so it is no surprise that many of her stories are based on historical incident.

Miss Bothwell first became interested in Sir Walter Raleigh's colonists when she was asked to do a book about them for the John C. Winston American Adventure Series and her *Lost Colony* was published in 1953. In LADY OF ROANOKE, Miss Bothwell continues her account and her own solution of this historical mystery, after a great deal of research, some of it on location in North Carolina.

Now a resident of New York City, Miss Bothwell was born and raised in Nebraska and has also lived in India, where she applied her American business training to management in two mission schools and a hospital. Though she now devotes full time to her writing, some leisure hours are spent in the reading of "who-dun-its" (which she also writes herself!) and in adding to her collections of stamps and American Pressed Glass.